"I'm tire[...]"

"Tired of running and hiding. I want to see you."

"That's what I want, too," he said. "It's what I need. I need to wake up next to you and hold you close."

"Nick, please," Ella begged. "It can't be like that for us until my life settles down. What you're describing is paradise."

"No, Ella, it's anywhere we're together."

"Not if the press is there, Nick. You have your future, your career. Another skirmish like that last one, and you might just as well forget about the State Department."

Ella knew that Nick was jeopardizing his career to be with her. She had to convince him that each time they were together would be bad for him, worse than the time before. If he couldn't be convinced, then the next step was up to her....

Dear Reader,

When two people fall in love, the world is suddenly new and exciting, and it's that same excitement we bring to you in Silhouette Intimate Moments. These are stories with scope, with grandeur. The characters lead the lives we all dream of, and everything they do reflects the wonder of being in love.

Longer and more sensuous than most romances, Silhouette Intimate Moments novels take you away from everyday life and let you share the magic of love. Adventure, glamour, drama, even suspense—these are the passwords that let you into a world where love has a power beyond the ordinary, where the best authors in the field today create stories of love and commitment that will stay with you always.

In coming months look for novels by your favorite authors: Maura Seger, Parris Afton Bonds, Linda Howard and Nora Roberts, to name just a few. And whenever you buy books, look for all the Silhouette Intimate Moments, love stories *for* today's women *by* today's women.

Leslie J. Wainger
Senior Editor
Silhouette Books

Anna James

Stairway to the Moon

Silhouette Intimate Moments
Published by Silhouette Books New York
America's Publisher of Contemporary Romance

SILHOUETTE BOOKS
300 East 42nd St., New York, N.Y. 10017

Copyright © 1988 by Shannon Harper and Madeline Porter

ISBN: 0-373-07255-4

First Silhouette Books printing September 1988

Printed in the U.S.A.

Books by Anna James

Silhouette Intimate Moments

Edge of Love #13
Her Own Rules #38
Love on the Line #65
The Venetian Necklace #104
Nina's Song #115
Images #135
The Reluctant Swan #147
The Dream Makers #167
Passage to Zaphir #207
Stairway to the Moon #255

Silhouette Special Edition

Their Song Unending #371

ANNA JAMES

spends most of her time in either Atlanta, Georgia, or
Los Angeles, California. She has written many different kinds of romances—from historicals to contem-
poraries, as well as numerous Gothics. When she's not
traveling or writing she enjoys tennis, the theater, long
walks on the beach and her three incompatible cats.

Chapter 1

Laughter drifted down the halls of the Cody Butler Wing at Children's Hospital. It came from the physical therapy gym, and it didn't show any signs of letting up as Ella Butler tried to recover her balance. For a moment she seemed about to succeed. Then she reached for the chalk on the hopscotch square, grabbed it in one hand, tottered on the opposite foot and fell, her long brown hair fanning out on the exercise mat.

"You look like some kind of giant bug, Ella," one of the kids in her class declared, "with your arms and legs going in every direction and your hair all wild."

The other children were laughing too hard to add their comments, and Ella, now right side up but still sitting on the mat, could only scowl at them in mock anger.

"I was never known for my agility at these kinds of games," Ella admitted. She managed to stand up, straighten her white hospital coat, retie the ribbon that held back her hair and regain some of her composure. "That doesn't mean those of you who are in the advanced section can't do better. You try, Donnie."

Donnie was about seven years old, with a face full of freckles and a wide grin. He managed to get through a round of hopscotch before falling, and his feat was rewarded with applause from the other kids.

"Maybe you should just *tell* us how to do the next exercise, Ella," one of the older kids suggested, "instead of showing us."

"Well, you're in luck," Ella replied as she glanced at her watch, "because I'm not going to do either. Class is over. You'll just have to wait until next time to see what fabulous exercise I come up with."

"Don't forget to practice up on it," the older boy suggested.

In response, he got a display of fast footwork from Ella.

"Hey, maybe boxing's your line," he said with a laugh as Ella tousled his hair, received some last-minute hugs from the little kids and finally managed to get back to the staff office, where she collapsed on the first available chair.

"Whew," Ella gasped as Dr. Susan Dunne followed her in. "I think I prefer therapy with kids on crutches to this class in hand-to-eye coordination. If I have to teach them cartwheels I'm going to be in real trouble."

Susan laughed. "You're doing a great job with both classes, Ella, but I'm beginning to think you're working too hard. You look very tired."

"If I am, it's not because of the hospital. Being with the kids gives me a focus in life."

"Well, you've been a godsend to us, not just for underwriting the Cody Butler Wing but for volunteering so much time to the kids."

Ella answered honestly. "It was Cody's money and the wing's a fitting memorial for him, but the rest is all for me, Susan. I love being with the kids and helping in whatever way I can."

Susan sat down at the desk, adjusted her wire-framed glasses on the tip of her nose and smoothed back her graying hair. "Other women in your situation—the widow of a man who was both wealthy and famous—would be satisfied with making financial donations, but you've kept Cody's memory alive with your hard work." Susan and her husband were staff doctors at the hospital.

Ella answered thoughtfully, "In many ways it's as if he's still alive."

"I know. I can hardly believe two years have passed," Susan responded. "They've been difficult for you, Ella."

"But productive, too."

"I'm constantly amazed at how much you've learned, especially in pediatrics. I don't know how the nurses ever managed without you."

"I really love working with the newborns," Ella said. She tried to keep the pensive tone from her voice, but she wasn't entirely successful.

A long silence followed, which was interrupted at last by the sharp ringing of the telephone. Susan picked it up, responded briefly and told Ella, "Your car's at the side exit, but hang around a little while longer. The Jones baby is going home today."

"Oh," Ella sighed.

"I know. We'll miss her, but she's ready. Weighs six pounds at last. I thought maybe you'd like to see her off, since you were responsible for at least a couple of those pounds, but if you're too tired..."

"I wouldn't miss it for the world. Besides, I can rest up during the next two weeks on my vacation."

"A well-deserved one, too, even though I'll miss you."

"There's a solution to that. You and Doug come along," Ella suggested impulsively.

"If only..."

"Why not? You could at least fly over for a long weekend."

Susan was shaking her head. "Any other time, maybe, but not with the conference coming up next week. Doug would never be able to get away. You know how excited he is about hosting all those representatives of child care clinics from around the world."

"It's going to be a great conference. I'd like to attend it myself."

"You need the time off, Ella. We'll record everything and save all the information for you. Meanwhile, come on," she said, reaching for her hospital coat, "It's time for the Jones baby's farewell party."

* * *

More than an hour later, an exhausted but happy Ella Butler slipped out the side door of the Cody Butler Wing and into the back seat of a silver-gray limousine. The long car made its way through the traffic on La Cienega Boulevard while Ella closed her eyes and tried to lose herself in the classical music that played softly on the stereo. As they approached Laurel Canyon, the chauffeur's voice coming over the intercom interrupted the music.

"We're going into La Casa the back way, Mrs. Butler. There were some fans at the gate when I left."

"That's fine, Cal," Ella responded emptily. There were usually fans at the gates of La Casa. It had been that way when Cody was alive; it remained that way after his death. He'd been more than a superstar. One of the few entertainers to find success in movies, television and theater, he'd still left time to tour in concert. It was *that* Cody Butler the fans adored, the lanky young man with the gravelly voice, dressed in a blue workshirt and jeans, singing to them of broken hearts and broken dreams.

Ella had shared ten years and more with Cody on his roller coaster of fame until that day it all ended, suddenly, horribly, in a red Lancia. Cody's car had careened off the road, turned over a dozen times and crashed in a ball of fire at the bottom of the canyon. He'd been alone, and he'd been drinking. The media had a field day playing up the alcohol content of his body, but it hadn't fazed the fans. Cody Butler was their ideal; he could do no wrong. In death he was still larger than life, and Ella was still part of the legacy, all that his fans had left.

Or not quite all. There was La Casa, the luxurious estate tucked into the hills above Los Angeles, surrounded by a high stone fence and a wrought-iron gate that was guarded twenty-four hours a day.

Ella sighed as the limo climbed the canyon road. She'd kept hoping that as time passed the fans would find another idol to take Cody's place. That hope wasn't shared by Cody's manager, Art Newcombe, who perpetuated the legend, insisting that Ella take her place on the pedestal as *Cody's widow*, a substitute idol for the fans. Despite the continuing attention, despite Art, Ella tried to keep a low profile. She'd made a place for herself at the hospital, where she was just Ella to the kids, but when she ventured out in public she was always recognized, and when she returned to La Casa, they were always there—the watchers.

Now that she was thirty-one, Ella's life was circumscribed. She lived behind walls that often felt as confining as a prison, but to leave the protection of those walls for good would take a courage she didn't yet possess. Ella sighed again. Susan was right; she was tired, but the exhaustion wasn't physical. She was tired of being Cody's widow.

The limo turned onto a side road that led to the back of the estate. It, too, was closed in by an iron gate, but inside the private compound there was no need for a guard. The chauffeur stopped the car and pushed a button. The gate swung open to let them through.

"I'll get out here, Cal," Ella said. She wanted to walk for a few minutes, and the woods that surrounded the estate were cool and comforting in the late afternoon. No one could see her there, although she'd seen helicopters fly very low, buzzing over the pool and tennis courts for a glimpse of Ella Butler in her shorts or bathing suit.

Ella walked along the path between the guest cottages and the pool and took off the huge dark glasses that she used to hide her deep blue eyes from view when she was in public. Although she had her privacy here, she'd reached the point where she preferred putting the glasses in place and going out in the world. If only the world weren't so anxious to have a piece of her; if only the world were a place where she could be herself. So far she'd found that place at the hospital, but even there the association with Cody was strong; it was *his* wing, built with *his* money.

"Good afternoon, Mrs. Butler." A voice startled Ella, then she saw the gardener looking over a mass of the begonias that grew in profusion around the estate. "It's a beautiful day," he said with a grin.

"Yes, it is, Joe," Ella replied. "And your flowers make it even more beautiful." This was her life, and these were the people she saw from day to day: the gardeners, the chauffeur, the guards, her maid and all the others who took care of La Casa and Ella. Controlling them all, even though he didn't live on the estate, was Art Newcombe.

She crossed the brick patio and went into the back hall of the huge Spanish-style house that Cody had whimsically and irreverently named La Casa. *The house.* Ella's footsteps were muted on the thick carpet as she made her way along the hall to the front of the house. She'd started up the wide staircase when another voice called out to her.

"*Señora...*"

"Yes, Juanita?"

"Señorita Stoddard is in your office. She has *los billetes*."

"Thanks, Juanita." Ella quickened her steps to the second floor and hurried down another long hallway toward her office. Nikki had finally gone by the travel agency to pick up their tickets, along with all the brochures from the resort. Their carefully planned vacation trip was about to become a reality, two weeks in the South Pacific away from Hollywood, away from Cody's fans and La Casa. Ella couldn't wait.

On the other side of the globe, where a murky river twisted like a serpent toward the city, Nicholas Manning was also thinking about his vacation. It would be a long and well-deserved one, for he'd been overseas more than three years.

Bangkok was a stopping-off place on his way home. Nick had always been comfortable here, and even though the heat was oppressive, it was no worse than in many other capitals he'd lived in or visited.

Tonight the city streets were filled with crowds of strollers. They meandered along the canals, trying to catch a breath of breeze, but even at ten o'clock in the evening the air was still hot and sticky with the hint of rains just ended or about to begin.

Nick sat at a table on the terrace of the elegant Palais Hotel, an icy glass of Campari before him. He was dressed in cotton trousers and a short-sleeved shirt.

An older man joined him and ordered a cold beer. "Well, my friend," he said, "how does it feel to be going home?"

Nick's eyes widened with interest, and a smile spread over his tanned face. "Like Christmas, the Fourth of July and my birthday all rolled into one."

Gavin Reid, Nick's superior at the U.S. State Department, gave an answering smile. "How long has it been?"

"You know the answer to that as well as I do, Gavin. You people are the ones who've kept me here *three years*," he said emphatically.

"You've had some leaves during that time," Gavin reminded him.

"Mmm. After two years in Pakistan I had a short home leave when my father was in the hospital. Last year I managed to sneak in a couple of weeks in Rome. Hardly what I was promised when I joined the Foreign Service."

"We needed you, Nick. Believe me, the Secretary knows how tough it was for us in Pakistan, caught in the middle between the government and the Afghanistan refugees. Lahore isn't one of our most desirable posts, I'll admit."

"Lahore is a good post," Nick countered. "I just didn't spend much time there. The Afghanistan border was another matter."

"Well, you did a fine job on that tour of duty, and believe me, it won't be overlooked."

Nick was hardly listening. Instead, his mind had flipped back in time, paused briefly in Lahore, where he'd lived in comparative comfort in a large house with a competent staff and a superb cook. The work there had not been easy; in fact, it had been frequently frustrating and sometimes dangerous. Good meals had lightened the work load; so had receptions at other embassies, a few casual flirtations, even one satisfying love affair.

The border had been another matter, a living hell. Nick remembered the camps, the suffering of sick and confused women and children caught up in a conflict they had nothing to do with and didn't understand. He'd done what he could, helped in his own way through his country's State Department. It had never been enough, and it had sapped his energy, taken so much from him mentally and physically that he'd been ready to leave. He did deserve a rest.

"Yes," he said, interrupting his own reverie, "I've had enough hardship for a while. It'll be good to get back home." Home. He couldn't help smiling at the word. It brought visions of Virginia, rolling fields of green surrounded by whitewashed fences and hedges of multiflora rose, a tall brick house with gracefully fluted columns. It seemed like centuries since he'd spent a lazy afternoon drinking mint juleps on the lawn at Fox Haven.

"You'll have a couple of months," Gavin was saying.

"Three, I believe, is customary," Nick corrected him.

"Depending on what is next in line for you." Gavin took a sip of beer. His smile created additional crevices in his weathered face. "I believe the Secretary has something special in mind after your debriefing."

Nick raised a dark eyebrow.

"What would you say to an ambassadorship?"

Nick frowned in disbelief.

"It does happen, you know. Career officers are appointed to ambassadorial posts."

"Occasionally," Nick agreed as he nodded toward the waiter for another round of drinks.

"You've had fifteen years of good, tough service. You've eased a great deal of suffering among people, as well as tension between governments. You're the kind of man who gives our country a good name on all levels. In short, you're due, my friend."

Nick didn't answer for a long time. He was thinking about his years of service. He *was* dedicated, but he was also ambitious. Nick Manning liked to be where he could make a difference; he liked to be near the center of power. An ambassadorship would suit him well.

"What do you think?" Gavin asked.

"I think we're being a little premature. I'll make my decision when I've heard the offer."

"It's a sure thing," Gavin predicted.

"A man could go broke very quickly betting on sure things in government," Nick commented.

Gavin laughed. "You've got me there."

"Besides, all I'm thinking about now are my two weeks on Balboa. I hope the resort is all you've made it out to be."

"All that and more," Gavin insisted. "Quite a few of our people use it as a hideaway. It boasts excellent accommodations in beautiful surroundings. All very discreet. The resort caters to people who want R and R and nothing else. Serenity is what it's all about."

"I certainly could use some of that."

"You'll get it, my friend, and all without a fuss. Nobody'll bother you, I guarantee. Unless, of course, you want them to. I hear the island women are among the loveliest in the South Pacific."

Nick laughed. "An exotic island beauty isn't my fantasy at the moment."

"Don't tell me you're a man without fantasies."

"None that you'd be interested in."

"Try me," Gavin urged with a grin.

"Would you believe a nice American girl, easygoing and uncomplicated, who wants to meet a nice American boy?"

Gavin laughed. "Not for a minute. You're not describing the type of woman who could hold the interest of a man as complicated as you."

"You overestimate me."

"I don't think so. If you wanted the easy life, you'd go home and help your family run Fox Haven. Virginia can always use another gentleman farmer, but you'd get wanderlust before a month was out. It's happened before."

"I was younger then," Nick countered.

"You're still young, my friend. Thirty-seven is just beginning in your field. You have a long future ahead, and you're not going to spend it on the simple life. As

for the simple woman, no way. You're much too sophisticated. No all-American girl for you.''

"Regardless of what you say, she remains my
dream.''

"Suit yourself. Maybe you'll find that dream on
Balboa.''

Pamphlets and brochures from Balboa resort were
spread across Ella's office desk; her secretary's five-
foot-eleven-inch frame was stretched out nearby on a
chaise.

Nikki Stoddard had been Ella's friend since the very
first days of Cody Butler's fame. A beautiful girl with
red hair and green eyes and a perfect long-legged figure, she'd joined Cody's show as a dancer in his
backup act. She and Ella were the same age, and
they'd become instant friends even though Ella was as
innocent and protected as Nikki was worldly and in-
dependent.

Cody had approved of Nikki. She'd never deferred
to him; often she'd disagreed, even talked back. In a
world of sycophants, he'd found that refreshing. He'd
thought Nikki had style; she was good for Ella.

"You'll just flip over these pictures," Nikki said
when Ella burst into the room. "They've sent us a
whole new batch, and the place is more beautiful than
I'd imagined.''

Ella reached for a stack of photos and sat down on
the chaise beside Nikki. They'd spent weeks poring
over information from resorts all over the globe,
driving the travel agent crazy with their indecision.
Finally, Ella had made the choice on the basis of Bal-

boa's isolation. Nikki had agreed. They both needed
peace and quiet.

Ever since she'd quit show business to become Ella's secretary, Nikki had kept the world from Ella's
door. She handled requests for interviews, invitations
to celebrity parties and charity balls and answered the
mail with the help of a staff that was almost as large
as it had been when Cody was at the height of his
popularity. Nikki also had the difficult task of acting
as a liaison between Ella and Art, who had his own
ideas about the image Cody's widow should project.

Ella knew that her friend needed this vacation, that
Nikki was secretly excited, although she looked casual, relaxing comfortably in the room she and Ella
had decorated together. The chaise was covered in a
pattern of pale turquoise and peach with the wicker
frame painted turquoise to match the other furniture
in Ella's office, all of it wicker, with bright covers and
pillows. The floors were white tile covered with scat-
ter rugs; plants abounded. It was a room unlike any in
the rest of the overdecorated house. It was Ella's favorite, cool and tasteful—her refuge.

Turning her attention back to the photographs, Ella
declared, "This looks better than I'd dreamed."

"Scrumptious is the word for it," Nikki suggested.

Ella gave her friend an appreciative look. "I'm so
glad you're going with me. Thanks, Nik."

"Oh, it was really a difficult decision. I mean, to
leave this huge traffic jam under smoggy skies they call
L.A. for a trip to the South Pacific is a hardship, I
must tell you, Ella."

Ella laughed. "What do the boys think about our plans?"

"They're excited—and they were jealous. So I promised they could go on the school-sponsored trip to Hawaii over the holidays. The jealousy subsided very quickly, let me tell you."

Nikki's two sons attended a boarding school in the San Gabriel Mountains. Even though they'd been in private school since Nikki's marriage to an itinerant actor had broken up, the boys were very close to their mother, and she visited them frequently. Ella usually went along. The school was another place where her anonymity was assured.

"I promised we'd drive up and tell them all about the trip as soon as we got back," Nikki continued.

"I won't have any trouble keeping that promise." The boys had been favorites of Ella's since the days she baby-sat for them when Nikki was on tour. "My love for kids started with those two," Ella said unabashedly.

"You're a born mother, as I've told you from the beginning, but I was the one who ran off and got married at seventeen and had kids right away. Me, a dancer, for goodness' sake, out on the road half the time, dragging them along or leaving them at La Casa. Let's face it. You ended up being their mother. I'm surprised they ever got it all straight."

"They're show-business kids; there's no doubt about that," Ella admitted.

"Lucky ones, to have a substitute mother like you. The question is, when are you going to become a real

mother? Or a real wife? Or even a real girlfriend, for
that matter?''

Ella tried to ignore those questions, but hiding her
feelings about children was more difficult with Nikki
than it had been with Susan, because Nikki knew her
too well.

''When you find a man, I guess,'' Nikki said, answering all the questions for Ella. ''Which you can't
do hidden behind the walls of La Casa.''

''You have a point there.'' Ella gathered the photographs and brochures from Balboa, not wanting to
dwell on her solitary life. ''However, we're breaking
out of these walls in a few days....''

Thoughtfully, she put the Balboa folder in her desk
drawer. ''I wonder what kind of people will be at the
resort.''

''Rich,'' Nikki said automatically. ''Spoiled, probably. Celebrities who don't want to be overwhelmed by
their public. Not just movie stars, though. They cater
to government and business types, too. Now, those are
men of another kind altogether.''

Without responding, Ella sank into a comfortably
padded wicker chair, but she'd kept out a few of the
pictures, which she flipped through again.

''Look carefully,'' Nikki urged her. ''There are
some very attractive men in those shots. Indicative of
all the ones who'll be there next week.''

''All of them prepared to fall madly in love with
you.''

''I'm taken,'' Nikki said, stretching back luxuri-
ously on the chaise.

''Frank's going to miss you, too.''

"I know," Nikki purred, "but he'll have all those textbooks to keep him company, and if I'm lucky, he'll finish his paper before I get home so we can have a few days to ourselves. Then it'll be back to the library stacks."

"You aren't complaining, are you?"

"Heavens, no. Whenever he gets his nose out of his books, my college professor is a match for any man. I don't even mind the ink smudges and chalk dust. They come with the territory. Besides," she said seriously, "it's great to be in love with a man who likes my mind as well as my body. Now the object is to find someone with those sensibilities for you, and we certainly won't find him around here in Tinseltown."

"True," Ella agreed. "I've known that for a long time. Men in L.A. fall into two categories: the ones who are so intimidated by Cody and his memory that they treat me like a living memorial, almost as if I were a marble statue and not a real human being . . ."

Nikki nodded in sympathetic agreement. "And the other category?"

"Even worse. They're out to use me or, more specifically, to use Mrs. Cody Butler to get into the movies or close a record deal. If they're seen with me they'll be photographed, written up in the columns and—presto—instant stardom."

"They're creeps," Nikki said. "But there's another group, and it's pretty big. As big as the whole country, in fact. It's all the men outside Hollywood."

"Mmm," Ella mouthed noncommittally.

"Explain that noise."

"They're just as bad."

"Impossible."

"Want to bet?" Ella kicked off her shoes, plumped up the pillows behind her and threw her legs over the arm of the chair. "The rest of the world is more intimidated by Cody than this town ever was. They think he was some kind of god and worship me as his widow, or they think he was some kind of devil...."

"And?"

"I don't know. I guess they consider me at worst a witch, at best a poor, ignorant, misused woman." She added with decided understatement, "Either way can't make for a healthy relationship."

"I guess not, but there must be a charming, attractive man somewhere who never heard of Cody Butler."

"No such species exists," Ella declared.

Nikki was silent for a while, rearranging herself on the chaise, a thoughtful frown creasing her forehead. "Which makes it a little difficult for you to become a wife and mother. Even though my two can sometimes drive a normal person crazy, you still want kids, don't you?"

"Dozens, and all because of your two. And the kids at the hospital."

"Then we've got a problem. It's not possible to have a baby without a man."

"Oh, yes, it is," Ella said with a giggle.

"Ella, you wouldn't—"

Ella was laughing outright. "Good Lord, no. I could never consider anything like artificial insemination. It's too impersonal."

"But not unheard-of," Nikki said, reconsidering for a moment and then shaking her head decisively. "No, there's just one solution, and that's to forget about a 'meaningful relationship' and concentrate on making a baby.''

"Nikki!"

"If you want a baby badly enough," Nikki continued, undaunted. "You'll just have to grab hold of the best-looking guy in Balboa and mingle your genes with his."

Ella threw a pillow at Nikki, who avoided it easily. "I never could be so calculating. You know that. Besides, with this strange and irregular cycle of mine, I'd never figure out the right time to get pregnant anyway. That's one of the reasons Cody and I—" Ella broke off. Nikki knew all about that; she also knew that in the last years, when Cody's life had begun to take on self-destructive aspects, Ella's childlessness had become a blessing.

Ella put those thoughts aside and blinked back the tears that had threatened for a moment to fill her eyes. "Aren't I something?" she said as much to herself as Nikki. "A little girl from Tyler, Texas, widow of one of the most famous men in the world. How did I ever end up this way, Nikki?"

"Just plain luck, honey."

The two women looked at each other and began to laugh, but Ella couldn't keep the memories from flooding in. She knew Nikki was remembering, too, the early years when everything had seemed to go Cody's way, when fame and adulation had been out there to enjoy. Enjoy it he had; all of them, the whole group, had basked in the light of his success.

"It was good at first," Ella mused aloud.

"Yes," Nikki agreed.

"I really loved him, Nikki."

"I know you did, and you were special to him, the only one he ever needed or trusted."

"Why couldn't I make him happy?" Ella asked not for the first time.

"No one could have made Cody happy, Ella. Your life revolved around him, and still that wasn't enough. He was going so fast he couldn't stop. The only thing that ever stopped Cody was death. He met that head-on."

Ella heard the truth in what Nikki said. She'd heard it before; she'd always known it. She'd been a part of Cody for more than ten years. Now it was time to become a person in her own right, not Mrs. Cody Butler, but Ella.

"Enough of this talk about the past," Nikki said suddenly. "Let's get back to the subject at hand: Balboa. Whatever happens there—and I have a feeling it'll be something good—we have to be dressed for the occasion." She got to her feet and, pulling Ella after her, headed down the hall. "We'll go through your closets and put together a wardrobe for the trip."

"I don't have much in the way of resort wear."

"Good," Nikki said. "That'll give us an excuse to go shopping. This is going to be a fabulous holiday, and you're going to look even more smashing than usual."

Chapter 2

Ella sat on the porch of the bungalow she and Nikki shared at Paradise Cove. Sunlight filtered through the slatted roof onto the book in her lap. She stopped reading long enough to shift position, and then let her eyes close as she thought about the past two weeks. Their vacation was drawing to an end, and it had been just what she'd hoped for from the moment she'd looked out of the airplane window onto the chain of islands flung like emeralds across the turquoise sea. The resort, snuggled around a three-mile curve of pure white sand, was everything its brochures claimed.

The Balboa Islanders had gained their independence from England and had struggled to make it as exporters of coconut and copra but had barely survived until a group of investors created the resort and tourism became its number-one business.

The islanders were now prosperous, but Ella suspected that those who hadn't come to work on the resort, the men, women and children who lived on the other, smaller islands, were less lucky. She'd wanted to see for herself but hadn't done so yet because the motor launches were always too crowded. Though none of the guests had paid special attention to Ella, she continued to avoid large groups.

With a little sigh she looked around at her own private paradise, which was shaded by coconut palms, scented by the perfume of exotic flowers and cooled by the soft trade winds. Bright orange bougainvillea dripped from the porch trellises. Ella had picked a huge bunch of blossoms, which were arranged in a vase on the glass-topped table.

"You're a vision surrounded by orange," Nikki said as she came out the front door of the bungalow and lifted her camera.

Ella looked up at that instant and stuck out her tongue defiantly.

Ignoring the response, Nikki advanced the film and got another shot.

"I believe you've photographed me in every setting on this island," Ella said, and went back to her book.

"Except in the shower," Nikki corrected as she tried another angle, "which I may do soon, because there, at least, you won't have your nose in a book."

Ella laughed and put the book aside. "I guess I have done an inordinate amount of reading on this trip, but it's been so peaceful and quiet that I couldn't resist catching up."

"Catching up? Ella, you've already read more than any ten people I know, including my erudite professor. Of course, you always were a reader, even back in the early days.''

"To close the gap in my education,'' Ella explained. ''You know that.''

"You've certainly done that. Why, you're an authority on just about every subject. The Marleys were impressed with you at dinner last night.''

Ella laughed. ''They were probably surprised that I could even read.''

"That, too,'' Nikki admitted as she dropped into a porch chair beside Ella. ''Nobody expects the widow of Cody Butler to be into books, not to mention into bridge. You and the colonel really trounced us.''

"The colonel's a fantastic partner. Too bad you drew his wife—who can't stop chatting long enough to finesse a queen.''

"Oh, that reminds me. There's going to be an eight-table tournament tonight with some super prizes. Why don't you join in?''

Ella shook her head. ''I don't think so.''

"Now, I'm not going to lecture you, Ella,'' Nikki said, starting to do just that while Ella only half listened. She'd heard it all before: too many long walks on the beach, too many books consumed, not enough mingling with the other guests.

"That's the worst part,'' Nikki was saying, and Ella quickly tried to catch the last of the lecture. ''You confine yourself to small groups, two couples at the most.''

"It's safer,'' Ella admitted.

"But it's not as much *fun.* You're a prisoner in L.A., so why not enjoy yourself here, at least in your last couple of days? I guarantee you'll be no more than a face in the crowd, if you'll just get up the nerve to go out in a crowd."

"I don't know," Ella hedged.

"Honey, this place is filled with the famous and will-be-famous and already-have-been-famous. They all get out and mingle. I saw the prime minister of Canada and his wife at the pool party, and no one gave him a second look. The guests aren't about to intrude, and there are no reporters in sight, not even a photographer sneaking around in the bushes."

"Except for you," Ella reminded her with a smile.

"I don't sneak around," Nikki said, taking mock offense. "I just thrust my camera right out there and snap. No one seems to mind. I suppose they can guess my amateur status. But I'm the only one, so you're free to get out and enjoy yourself."

"I *am* enjoying myself, just not in crowds. I don't want to take a chance on being approached. It's been perfect so far, being able to forget who I am. I actually woke up this morning thinking I was just another person. I took a long walk on the beach all alone with no one watching over me. It was wonderful."

"That's the other thing. I haven't mentioned this before, but—"

It was Ella's turn to interrupt. "Don't tell me there's some part of this lecture that you haven't covered."

Nikki continued, unperturbed. "Exercise is fine, but you play tennis only with the pro, when there's mixed doubles going on all the time. You learned to snorkel, but you haven't even gone on the motor launch trip to Kikao, where the water's supposed to be perfect."

Ella thought about that for a moment. "I've wanted to go over there, not just for the snorkeling but to visit the little villages and see what life's like on one of the other islands."

Nikki sighed. "I might have known there was a humanitarian motive behind it, but whatever gets you going is okay with me. Will you promise to go this afternoon?"

"Nikki, I never said—"

"Promise."

"Okay. I promise, if you go with me."

"Not a chance. I'm practicing up for the tournament tonight with all my Brit friends. We're drawing partners, so keep your fingers crossed that I get the colonel."

"Nikki—"

"No, Ella, you're going without me. You promised. Get your gear together, put on your bathing suit and show off that gorgeous tan."

Nick noticed her the moment she got into the motor launch. She wasn't the most beautiful woman he'd seen at Paradise Cove. There had been plenty of those, including film stars, models and the mistresses of wealthy businessmen. No, she was different, so different that for a moment he was jarred by her. He'd never have admitted this to Gavin, but she looked exactly like the woman of his fantasies. He forced himself to look away, and when he looked back she'd disappeared. Momentarily panicked, Nick moved through the passengers to the front of the launch, and there she was, sitting in the prow by herself.

Ordinarily he wouldn't have hesitated to approach a pretty woman who was obviously alone, but something stopped him this time, in spite of the attraction. She looked unsure of herself, a little shy, and he had the feeling she'd be offended if he spoke to her, so he held back.

But he couldn't stop looking. Other passengers had made their way to the prow, and he was just one of the crowd, able to stare at her unnoticed. Her light brown hair was pulled away from her face, but a few strands had come loose and fallen across her eyes. He watched as she brushed them back carelessly, and he felt a little ache inside at the loveliness of the gesture.

Then he turned away again, advising himself to relax. He wasn't a kid smitten by a sudden fatal attraction. Yet that's exactly how he felt. He looked back, relieved that she was still there. She had a beautiful tan, not too dark, but golden brown, just the color of her hair when it caught the sunlight. She looked trim in her white shorts, but not thin; her long legs were shapely. The shirt she wore was brightly flowered and a little baggy, a style he'd noticed since his return to civilization but hadn't cared for until now. On her it looked very sexy, even though it left almost everything to the imagination. He let his work overtime.

An enthusiastic couple planted themselves at the rail beside Nick, discussing the trip and completely blocking his view of the woman. He tried to get away but was soon captured in conversation. Finally extricating himself, he moved away, only to find that he was almost face-to-face with her. Because he could think of nothing else to do, he smiled.

When she saw the smile, Ella felt the breath catch in her throat. She'd never seen teeth so white and even, eyes so dark, flashing in a face that was deeply tanned. For a moment she thought he was going to speak, and then, as quickly as he'd appeared before her, he passed on, moving to the other side of the prow, greeting another group of people, turning away from her for the first time and not turning back.

Ella forced herself to look out to sea. The sky was so darkly blue that it was almost impossible to tell where sea ended and sky began. The breeze caught in the waves, created patches of whitecaps that imitated the sky's white clouds. It was as if the sky were a mirror that reflected the sea. Ella watched this phenomenon, which at any other time would have fascinated her, without really seeing it.

She'd noticed the man staring at her when he first boarded the launch. Thinking he recognized her and trying to avoid celebrity status, she'd quickly moved to the other end of the boat. When she looked up again, there he was. She tried each time not to notice and escape back into her thoughts, but it had gotten more and more difficult. Then, when he smiled at her, standing only a few feet away, for a moment it had seemed as if they were the only two people on the boat, a part of the sea and sky, which today were also one.

The moment had passed, and now Ella looked back out to sea, wondering why he'd turned away so quickly. It didn't take long for her to figure it out: he'd recognized her, seen that she was Cody's widow and lost interest immediately. He was just like all the rest, intimidated—or awed—by who she was. Either way, it didn't matter. Ella didn't expect that she'd ever escape Cody's fame.

When the boat docked at Kikao, Nick stayed back until everyone had debarked, talking with the skipper of the little launch. Then he made his way slowly and without much interest to the bay, where the water was crystal clear and perfect for snorkeling. He carried his gear with him, but all of a sudden the sport didn't seem particularly appealing.

He knew why. For a moment there—no, more than a moment; almost an hour—he'd become entranced with a vision that was straight out of his fantasies. He'd gotten so close, closer than he'd meant to, and finally decided to introduce himself. That was when he'd seen that she was wearing a wedding band. He was too entranced by her to bother with polite conversation, and he had no intention of getting involved with a married woman, so he'd moved on and the boredom had returned.

It had actually set in a few days before, after he'd swam and sailed and danced and dined to the point of saturation and begun to think of cutting his vacation short and heading back to the States. He'd tried to put off the decision. Boredom wasn't a good sign, but it was a part of what always happened. His driving personality wouldn't let him relax; ultimately, restlessness set in.

The woman had provided a touch of excitement; that's all he would admit, although he knew there'd been more to it than that. Or so he thought, but when he arrived at the bay, he saw her again. Once more she was standing alone, away from the rest of the group that was already entering the water farther up the beach. She'd taken off her shorts and shirt and was wearing a simple one-piece bathing suit. Except that it wasn't so simple, not on her, anyway. It resembled the kind of suit a competition swimmer would wear, black, tight-fitting and no-nonsense. She looked like a million dollars in it.

As the other swimmers plunged into the bay, she walked along the waterline to a rocky spot farther down the beach. She was still carrying her gear but made no move to put it on. Nick shook his head a couple of times to get free of the fantasy he'd wrapped her in and spoke aloud. "What the hell," he told himself. She was alone; she looked nervous and unsure. It was time for him to put that ridiculous fantasy aside and help the woman learn to snorkel.

He walked across the fine powdery sand and stopped a few feet away from her. "Looks as though you're having second thoughts about going in."

She looked up at him, startled, and he was taken aback by her eyes. They were bluer than they'd seemed on the boat, blue and—innocent. That was the word. Innocent. He hadn't thought of that word or used it in a long time, certainly not to describe any of the women he'd known.

"Why don't you join the others?" He motioned toward the group of swimmers down the beach.

"No, I—"

Thinking again that she was afraid, Nick stepped closer. "Well, if you want a teacher, I've snorkeled hundreds of times, and I'd be glad to give you pointers."

"Dressed like that?" she asked, flashing a beautiful smile.

Only after he'd digested the smile did Nick realize he was still wearing his shirt and long pants. He laughed. "Where do I change?"

"Over there," she said, pointing toward a row of structures along the beach.

"I'll be right back. You go on in." He turned and then hesitated. "Or if you're afraid to go alone—"

"No, that's all right," she told him. "I'll meet you near the reef, but maybe I should know my teacher's name."

Nick put out his hand and tried to sound as impersonal as possible as she put her own slim hand in his. "I'm Nick."

"I'm Ella," she said, and flashed that brilliant smile again, before turning and heading toward the ocean, pulling on her mask as she walked.

He looked after her for a moment, a little perplexed that the woman he'd expected to be shy and hesitant had turned out to be very sure of herself. Shaking his head in puzzlement over her for the second time that day, Nick went into one of the lean-tos that served as dressing rooms and put on his bathing suit.

When he returned to the beach, she was already underwater near the reef. The water was so clear that he could see her as she swam—expertly, he noticed, the top of her snorkel skimming the surface. Nick stood for a long time at the water's edge, watching her and laughing at himself. He'd offered to teach Ella to snorkel, and there she was, out among the sea creatures, perfectly at home in the water.

Nick was both amused and confused. He couldn't help wondering why, since she was such an expert, Ella had seemed so shy, so unsure, staying far from the rest of the group. Yet when he'd intruded on her privacy, she hadn't seemed to mind. She was a puzzle, in reality more intriguing than in fantasy. But he wasn't going to solve the puzzle here on the beach; he might not solve it in the ocean either, but at least he'd be near her. Nick adjusted his mask, pulled on the fins and slipped into the water. Swimming strongly, he approached the reef, fitted the snorkel in place and stroked until he was just below the surface.

He and Ella swam alongside each other around the coral reef. Fishes of every shape and size darted in and out of the formations of pink, rose and purple coral, scattering as the two human forms approached. For a few seconds they had the water to themselves; then the schools of fish returned and joined in the swim, fluttering around, in and out of the lacy coral, sometimes in masses so thick they created a shimmering curtain of color that blocked out the light.

Intrigued and delighted by the coral and their sea companions, Nick and Ella stayed at the reef most of the afternoon, diving again and again and then coming up to blow the water from their snorkels before deciding on another spot to explore and submerging again.

As fascinated as he was by the sea life, Nick was equally delighted by the woman who swam by his side. Her arms and legs moved through the water gracefully; her body undulated, twisted and turned among the waving branches that created an underwater garden amid the coral. Swirling around her in the water, her golden-brown hair created another beautiful, shimmering effect.

"Had enough?" he asked when they emerged again.

"I could stay in the water all day. How about you?" she challenged him.

"Enough of the snorkeling," he said, tossing his equipment onto the reef. "But I'm ready for a race." He pointed toward a sandbar about a hundred yards out in the bay, and she nodded.

Nick gave Ella a head start and barely managed to catch up; they hit the sandbar swimming stroke for stroke. "You're an excellent swimmer," he said admiringly as they collapsed on the sand. "You must spend a lot of time at the beach."

Ella shook her head and answered simply, "I have a pool."

That put an end to his inquiry but not his curiosity. Ella was going to be a difficult woman to get to know. With each of his questions she seemed to draw a little more into herself. Not wanting to lose this elusive creature, he backed off, content to sit there beside her until they'd caught their breath and were ready for the return swim.

The beach was deserted as the afternoon shadows lengthened over the island. Nick and Ella changed back into their dry clothes in the makeshift dressing rooms and headed toward the nearest sign of activity, a thatch-roofed hut that served as a restaurant. Their group from Balboa was gathered at the tables in front, ordering drinks while they waited for the boat.

"Shall we join them?" Nick asked.

"Looks like a full house."

"We could walk down to the end of town and probably find some kind of store that sells soft drinks. Or is your husband waiting for you?" Unable to find an opening for that question all day, he'd fitted it in awkwardly because he had to know.

"My husband died two years ago." Ella saw that her response brought an embarrassed look to Nick's face, and she added quickly, "Let's walk until we find a store. I'd love to have a soft drink." She smiled and hoped she'd put him at ease. The afternoon had been so enjoyable she didn't want it to end back at the restaurant with their group from the boat. Not yet, anyway.

Nick smiled in return, and she relaxed. It was obvious now that he didn't know who she was; she wasn't about to tell him.

As they walked along, she tried to think of the last time she'd met someone who hadn't recognized her immediately. Even at Balboa, although they didn't make a thing about it, all the other vacationers knew, and just their knowing made her uncomfortable. With Nick it was possible for her to enjoy herself *as* herself. At the same time she couldn't help wondering who *he* was, this man, obviously an American but so completely out of the American scene.

When he'd first looked over at her on the boat, Ella had been magnetically drawn to him. That feeling hadn't ended when he'd turned away from her. Now he was back, almost like a figment of her imagination. Ella smiled. It all seemed so unreal.

"What's so funny?" Nick asked, bringing her back to reality. He *was* there beside her.

"I'm just thinking about how much I enjoyed this afternoon," she said, not quite lying—that was part of what she was thinking.

He stopped and looked down into her dancing eyes. "Who are you?" he asked only half jokingly. "Where do you come from?"

"My name's Ella Butler," she said, "and I come from Los Angeles." It was a lighthearted answer, in the spirit of his question, but it could have connected her with Cody. She waited, a little tense. He didn't react.

"My name's Nicholas Manning," he replied, "from Virginia. Let's have a cold drink."

They stopped in front of a concrete building, one side open to the breeze. It reminded Ella of a movie-set facade, which only added to the unreality that seemed to surround them.

Nick bought two cold bottled drinks, and they sat down at a rickety table under the partial shade of a coconut tree and drank them quickly, quenching their thirst. They laughed and didn't quite know why.

Nick looked back toward the dock. "The boat hasn't come yet. Would you like to explore?"

Ella's eyes lit up at that. In the late afternoon light the town was bathed in a soft glow, but there was a harshness among the houses lining the dirt street that the light couldn't hide. This was the island life that she'd been anxious to see, the life that wasn't pictured in brochures sent to prospective tourists.

They walked along, followed by a couple of kids who'd spotted them at the store, berry-brown boys of about eight or nine with hair and eyes as black as coal. The boys followed at a distance, stirring up the dirt with sticks, giggling behind their hands.

The houses off the main street were primitive, some of them no more than a few boards supporting a thatched roof. Colorful woven fabric hung from the doorways of the one-room structures, and children piled out, pushing the cloths aside, to watch Nick and Ella pass.

Farther along, a stream flowed by on the way to the ocean, and along its banks island women washed their laundry. Ella stopped to look at the scene, and the women, after an initial glance her way, resumed their work.

"I saw a water spigot at the corner," Ella said. "I wonder why they're washing clothes in the stream."

"They'd have to fill their tubs at the spigot and take them back to the house. There's something communal about washing at the stream."

Communal or not, it looked like very hard work, scrubbing the clothes against the rocks, Ella thought. "They don't have much, do they?"

"A roof over their heads," Nick said, "which is more than many people have."

Ella didn't answer, but a frown creased her forehead.

When they reached the end of the street, they went through a gate into a courtyard. Several buildings were grouped around the cobblestone area: a church, a school and a long, low structure that seemed empty and unused. Ella headed for it, watched by a group of kids sitting on the school house steps.

She looked inside the low building. It was fitted out, barely, as a medical clinic, but there was no one inside. A Closed sign hung on the doorknob. She turned to one of the kids who'd followed.

"Where is the doctor?" she asked.

"On the big island" was the response.

"How often does he come to Kikao?"

The boy shrugged.

Turning to another of the children, Ella repeated her question, but no one seemed to know the answer. Finally, one of the older girls chirped out, "He come every week."

Ella nodded as she joined Nick, who'd stood a little away, watching her interact with the kids. "A weekly doctor and a roof over their heads," she said, walking beside him out of the courtyard, "that's *not* very much, is it?"

He looked at her, thinking that most tourists would have considered the courtyard "quaint" if they thought about it at all. "No," he agreed, "It's not. But what little they have is a result of tourism. I imagine most of the family members work on the boats or in the shops that have sprung up since the big island was developed." As one of the boys who'd followed them earlier reappeared with a tray of coral beads, Nick added, "Even the kids benefit from us tourists."

"Buy, lady?" the boy asked, and Ella nodded with a laugh.

"I guess you're right," she said to Nick as she chose a pink coral necklace and held it up for him to see. "Isn't it beautiful?"

The little boy answered for Nick, grinning broadly, "Very, very beautiful. Only thirty-two namus."

"That's certainly reasonable," Ella said, reaching into her beach bag.

Nick put his hand out to stop her. "Please, let me buy it for you. But don't you want to bargain? That's the way here."

"No," Ella said adamantly. "I don't like to bargain. It cheapens the buyer and seller."

Nick didn't answer as he paid for the necklace, but he couldn't help thinking that the woman of his fantasy had turned out to be very special indeed.

As they walked back along the road, twilight descended upon them softly, giving the little village the glow it hadn't achieved in the afternoon sun.

"What time was the boat leaving?" Nick asked casually.

"I don't remember," Ella admitted. "You don't think it could have left without us, do you?"

"No such luck," Nick said, "but I guess we'd better pick up our pace a little."

It was too late. As they reached the restaurant, they saw that their fellow tourists had gone, and far out to sea, their launch was chugging away toward Balboa.

"There's an expression that sums up occasions like this: we missed the boat," Nick said with a laugh.

For a moment Ella was stunned, and then she joined in his laughter. "We're stranded on a tropical island. What an adventure!"

They were on the hill above the restaurant, and the waiter, hearing their laughter, came out to see what was happening. "At least it's not a *desert* island," Nick commented.

"What should we do?"

"Nothing. When they realize we're missing, they'll send a boat from the resort." He added with a grin, "I'm traveling alone, though, and no one will miss me for a couple of days."

"Well, my friend Nikki will alert the whole island and probably organize a search party."

Nick moaned. "I knew this was too good to be true." He glanced at Ella out of the corner of his eye and waited for that remark to register before saying, "We might as well have dinner while we wait." Giving a signal to the waiter, he took Ella's arm to help her down the hill. "I'd like to get to know my fellow castaway a little better."

Ella and Nick sat at a table outside under a thatched umbrella. Dusk had settled in and turned the ocean inky except for a shadow of magenta left by the setting sun. They ordered the rum and fruit drink that was an island speciality, salad and grilled mahi mahi.

While they waited for their meal, Nick watched Ella, who sat opposite him. She seemed very relaxed, and he cautioned himself to go carefully, not jarring her with questions that were so personal she would close up on him again. They talked about Balboa, and he asked her why she chose that particular resort.

"Because it's off the beaten path," she said truthfully.

He raised an eyebrow but didn't comment.

"I needed a hideaway where I could enjoy myself without being bothered by crowds."

"There are crowds on Balboa. There was a crowd on the boat," he suggested.

"I know," she answered quickly, "but the people here aren't intrusive."

Nick was more puzzled than ever, but he tried not to show it. He admitted to Ella that he liked the resort, but he didn't mention the boredom that had almost come over him. It was gone, anyway, now that he'd met Ella.

"You're different from most tourists," he said. "You seem to like getting away on your own and exploring."

"Don't you?"

"Yes, but it isn't always possible." He thought about the places his career had taken him, especially the last one, those long months at the border. "And sometimes it isn't pretty," he added.

Nick glanced away, but when he looked back she met his gaze directly, searching his face with her wide blue eyes. He knew at once that he was going to talk to her, really talk, tell her what he'd seen and where he'd been. He wouldn't have a light, frivolous conversation with Ella; she wasn't that kind of woman.

When the waiter came to clear away their dishes, Nick paid the bill and over coffee began to talk about his career, his life abroad, the good and the bad, and above all the past two years amid so much suffering.

As night descended, lanterns were strung around the patio, and Nick talked on. It was the first time he'd opened up in months. Even Gavin hadn't heard all that he told Ella, but he'd never had a listener like her before. She asked probing questions, and she understood his answers, however disjointed they were. She understood *him*.

"I've been away a long time," he said finally. "I guess I'm ready to go home."

"Where's home?" she asked.

"Virginia," he said. "Fox Haven."

"Fox Haven. What an unusual name. Is that a town?"

"No, it's my family's estate. The name goes back for several generations. Unlike most Virginians, my great-grandfather didn't believe in fox hunting. As the story goes, the foxes all hid out on his land. By my grandfather's time, the name was finally changed to reflect the family's feeling. Fox Haven."

"Manning tradition must go back a long way," she said.

"Yes, it does. In Virginia the family name remains important through generations, I suppose. What about your family?" he asked carefully, not wanting to intrude.

"I can't go back much further than my own parents. They were both from a small town outside Tyler, Texas."

"How did you get to Los Angeles?"

"With my husband," she said.

He hadn't even formed another question, when they heard the sound of a motor out in the bay.

"That could be our rescuers," Ella said. "I suppose we should go out to the dock."

"I suppose so," Nick said, but for a long time neither of them moved. The flickering lamplight seemed to make Ella even more mysterious and compelling. She'd walked into his life and completely mesmerized him. Nick didn't intend to let her slip away.

"Nick . . ."

"Yes?" he answered.

"We'd better go down to the dock so they can see us."

He stood up reluctantly and just as reluctantly walked beside her across the beach. The boat was just pulling in, its light creating yet another radiance in which Ella shone. He was suddenly determined to see her in every kind of light.

"Look—it *is* our boat," she said.

Nick thought he detected a little disappointment in her voice, but it could have been his imagination.

A line sailed out and dropped lazily onto the dock. Nick turned to Ella, and asked quickly, "Can I see you tomorrow?"

She nodded just as a voice from the boat called out, "Ella, here I am, your savior!" It was Nikki.

Chapter 3

Ella stood at the edge of the gathering. It was the
Saturday-night luau on the grounds of Balboa Resort, and everyone was there. She felt a little nervous
at the prospect of joining so many people, but she'd
promised to meet Nick and was determined not to
panic. Nikki had assured Ella that the guests at Balboa were as wary of publicity as she; on the boat trip,
she'd found that to be true. Now it was time to really
take the plunge. Still, she held back a few minutes,
waiting until darkness fell. Then, in spite of the light
from the flambeaux planted at intervals along the
lawn, Ella felt less conspicuous.

Smoke drifted up into the night air, its odors
tempting, and as Ella walked among the tables, a small
band began to play. The atmosphere was festive; no
one seemed to notice her, and she relaxed. Everything
was going to be all right. The ending to her day would

be perfect, just as her day had been, the first such experience she'd had in so many years that it was hard to remember.

The time with Nick had been *normal*. That was the first thing that struck her. Moreover, it had been exciting. That was the second thing, and it confused her, but it also made her happy. She couldn't explain the contradiction, and she didn't even worry about it. Nick would be here tonight, was probably already here, and they would end this perfect day together. That's all that mattered.

Making her way through the brightly garbed guests, she headed toward the pool, where she'd agreed to meet him. The men were wearing flamboyantly patterned shirts and white trousers, and the women wore variations of the native costume, a dress of printed material wrapped around the body, crossed over the breasts and tied behind the neck. The one Ella wore was blue and green; Nick had told her it brought out the vivid blue of her eyes when she'd tried it on at the resort shop that morning. She thought about his expression when he'd complimented her and blushed over the look that had probably been on her face, one of almost innocent appreciation. She'd had enough of sycophants in her life, of flatterers, but Nick meant what he said, and it made her happy.

As she passed tables laden with food and huge pitchers of tropical drinks, Ella was suddenly very hungry, and she realized that in their time together today she and Nick had never stopped to eat breakfast or lunch. They'd gone sailing in the morning, shopping in the afternoon and shared a coconut drink at a little stand on the beach somewhere along the way. She was ready for the luau.

"Ella, over here," Nikki called out from a table near the pool, not surprisingly a table for twelve. The gregarious Nikki was always in the middle of the largest and often the most interesting group. A little warily, Ella allowed herself to be introduced to all of them, only to find not a single eyelash batted at her name. They smiled, called out greetings, moved around in an effort to find room for her, but no one mentioned Cody.

Nevertheless, Ella declined to join the group. She was waiting for Nick, and she hoped that they would find a table just for the two of them. When he appeared and greeted the others, Ella thought for a moment that her hopes were unfounded. Whereas no one had made a fuss over her, quite the opposite was true when they were introduced to Nick.

Colonel Marley, Ella's recent bridge partner, reminded the others, "Manning's father was Ambassador to the Court of St. James's," and that brought immediate signs of recognition and remembrance from the mostly British group.

"I knew Manning Senior after the war when I was a military liaison for the Allies," the colonel told the table at large. "A brilliant man, quite a diplomat. Mrs. Manning was the prefect ambassador's wife, adept at handling every situation, and those postwar years in London were difficult for us all. Of course, you don't remember, my boy."

"No," Nick responded, "that was before I was born, but I've heard my father reminisce often about the London years."

"How are your parents?" the colonel inquired.

"Quite well. They've retired to their home in Virginia, but it's still pretty active around there."

"I imagine so, with so many members of your family in government. Your uncle is still in the Senate, isn't he?"

"It's beginning to look like a permanent job," Nick said with a laugh. He was responding easily and graciously to the questions, but the pressure of his hand on Ella's arm never diminished. She felt a connection with him even though she wasn't part of the conversation.

"What about you, Nick?" someone from the end of the table asked. "We hear you're in line for an ambassadorship."

Nick shook his head and answered evasively, "Then your hearing's better than mine."

Ella wondered. She was seeing another side of Nick, different from the one she'd come to like so very much during their time together. She'd seen him as a wonderfully kind and charming companion. He was, in fact, a powerful man; his was a world that she'd read about but never known, a world far from the one in which she'd grown up and even far from the one she'd shared with Cody. She hadn't sensed the power of Nick's world until now. Ella felt both awed and a little inferior standing beside him, listening to the talk and the compliments, unable to join in.

Nick was anxious for the conversation to end. He wanted nothing more than to get away to a table of their own where he could be alone with Ella, look at her, talk to her and, he hoped, later in the evening dance with her. He hadn't held her in his arms yet, and he'd have an excuse to do so on the dance floor. Finally he found an opening, politely refused the offer to join their group and ushered Ella to the buffet table, which offered roast suckling pig that had been turning on the open pit all day, barbecued chicken, grilled ham and every kind of fruit.

"I don't think I've ever been so hungry in my life," Nick admitted as he grabbed two plates and handed one to Ella. "Come on—let's load up."

Load up they did, taking their feast to a small table on the edge of the gathering. A waiter appeared from time to time to refresh their drinks, but otherwise they were alone, not quite a part of the festivities but still feeling a part of the gaiety. It was a bittersweet occasion, for tomorrow Ella would be leaving. Nick tried not to think about that, but he couldn't help himself as he watched her enjoying the piles of food on her plate with a gusto he admired. He barely knew her, and soon she would be gone; it all seemed a part of the fantasy, but then everything in his life had been transitory in recent years. Suddenly he felt a determination to put a stop to that, beginning with Ella.

She looked lovely in the dress that she'd tried on for him in the shop that morning. Nick had been knocked out when he'd first seen her in it, because the blue in the print was almost identical to the blue of her eyes. Almost but not quite. He didn't think her eye color could be duplicated; certainly he'd never seen eyes so beautiful, and he'd looked into quite a few blue eyes in his day. It wasn't just the color, he thought, but the hint of innocence, which seemed so incongruous in a grown woman and yet was there nevertheless.

He couldn't stop looking at her even as they both plunged into dinner, laughing at each other, though not in the least embarrassed by their gluttony. They paused occasionally to comment on the relative merit of the dishes but otherwise didn't put their forks down and lean back until the meal was finished and the waiter had come to clear away their plates and serve them coffee.

"Do you think we made a spectacle of ourselves?" Ella asked.

"Do you care?"

"Not in the slightest."

Nick laughed. "I like your spirit, Ella." In fact, he liked everything about her. Everything that he knew. He was sure he'd like the rest, all that he didn't know, if she'd open up and let him see more of Ella Butler. So far she'd let him do the talking about himself without reciprocating. He wanted to change that, but there was so little time.

"It's been a great day," he said. "So far." He planned for it to go on.

"Yes," she answered, "even if you had to spend a large part of it teaching me to sail."

"You're a quick study and a very good sport," he told her admiringly. "You learned to snorkel on your own, and you learned to sail with only a little help from me. Amazing. But I'm almost as amazed that, living in California, you never learned how to do either, especially when you swim like a fish." He waited for an explanation, but when it came it didn't satisfy him.

"The pool's just a few steps from my door."

She was still being evasive, he thought. "Did you also learn to dance by the pool?"

"You're teasing me now."

"Just a little," he admitted. "I expect when you were growing up you had more dancing partners than any girl in the state of Texas."

Ella seemed to stop and think about that for a moment before answering, "My husband was really my only partner."

"You didn't go dancing until you married?" Nick asked incredulously.

Ella laughed. "I married very young." Then without further explanation, she asked Nick, "Were you planning to dance with me this evening?"

It was Nick's turn to laugh. "Yes, that was my plan." He reached for her hand, and without hesitation, Ella rose and followed him across the yard to the wooden platform that had been set up as a dance floor amid the colorful foliage. The band segued from their energetic music into a slower beat as couples drifted away from their tables and into each other's arms.

For all practical purposes, Ella and Nick were just another one of those couples, but to Nick that was far from the case. Ella slipped into his arms easily, as if she belonged there. Yet he thought for an instant that he felt her tremble, but maybe he was the one who trembled. Holding her in his arms for the first time was certainly enough to make him do so. She was so slim, as light as air, and yet she didn't feel fragile. The curves of her body were soft and rounded, more delicious to hold than to admire. From the moment he'd seen her, he'd imagined holding her but somehow hadn't expected to. She was a surprise.

Nick thought he could feel her bare skin beneath his hands, her warm flesh through the material of the dress. He wondered if she was wearing anything under it. Moving his hand across her back to her waist and hip, he felt nothing but soft, firm flesh, and it made his head swim.

"You're a marvelous dancer," he said, just because he needed to talk to her in order to stop his imagination from working overtime. "Your husband must have been a good teacher."

"Yes, but no better than you were at teaching me to sail."

That pleased Nick even though he knew she was once more avoiding the subject, steering him away from talk about her husband. And to know her better, Nick would have to know something about that marriage, which had taken her at a young age from Texas to California and then, just two years ago, left her a widow. Had she been happy or miserable with him? Did she feel free now, or was she still in love with her husband's memory?

Those questions couldn't be answered here, obviously. "Would you like to take a walk on the beach?" he asked when the song ended.

Ella nodded, and he took her hand and led her across the long wide lawn to the powdery white sand of Paradise Cove. They removed their shoes, left them at the edge of the beach and walked hand in hand in the hard sand left by a retreating tide.

Nick had planned to talk to her, to find out what Ella Butler was all about, but words didn't seem to fit into this night on the beach; questions had no place in what he was feeling. Holding her hand as she smiled up at him was enough for now.

They stopped and looked out across the ocean, which was inky black except for a luminous trail cast by the light of the moon. It was narrow at the horizon and wider as it reached the shore.

"It looks like a stairway to the moon," Ella said, "almost real enough to climb."

"With you beside me, I probably could climb to the moon," Nick said. Any other time those words would have seemed overly romantic to him. Tonight they didn't. They fit the moment. He put his arm around Ella and looked down at her. Her blue eyes were deep and luminous. Her skin had a golden sheen. "You're very special, Ella," he said softly, "and very beautiful."

"It's the moonlight," she answered.

"No, the moonlight creates a magic stairway—that much I'll go along with—but you're beautiful enough even without the moonlight."

His words were followed by a long silence, during which there was no other sound except the rhythm of the incoming waves as they broke on the shore. Then, listening carefully, Nick could hear Ella's gentle breathing and, he thought, the pounding of his own heart. He touched her chin with his fingertips and tilted her face so he could look deeper into her eyes. He knew that he was going to kiss her and yet he hesitated, moving his fingers down her neck and along her shoulders, feeling her soft and pliant under his touch. Nick could hear his own breathing now; it was ragged and full of desire as he leaned down and pressed his lips to hers.

He felt a shock as their lips met, as if he'd been touched by fire. Hungrily he pulled her close, wrapping her in his arms, moving his mouth over hers, tasting, inhaling her sweetness. As his tongue invaded her mouth, Nick felt a shyness in her response. It seemed to flutter through her body. He heard a startled murmur deep in her throat. All that increased his desire for her. He kissed her harder, deeper, and then she responded in a way that he hadn't expected, returning his kiss with a passion that equaled his own.

Ella felt herself melting inside as her body fused with Nick's and her mouth was captured by his. She'd been first shocked by the intensity of his desire, then surprised by her own reaction, which turned so suddenly from perplexity to deep and growing need. She tightened her arms around his neck and clung to him, released from her shyness, not quite knowing what to expect and yet prepared to be lost in the kiss.

And she was lost; they both were, for a long interlude during which a cloud raced over the moon and temporarily obscured their luminous stairway.

"Oh, Ella," he said, "I've wanted to kiss you from the first moment I saw you."

Then she knew what she hadn't known before, that she'd wanted the same thing all along.

"I've wanted to kiss you," he repeated, "and hold you, and make love to you." He said the last phrase more boldly and felt her shyness return as she quivered a little in his arms. "Ella?"

She didn't answer. There was no answer that she could form, because while she wanted him and knew it could happen like this, quickly, passionately, she wasn't sure she could handle the magnetism. It was so

strong, stronger than the memory of Cody, and Cody
was the only man she'd ever been with. Because of
that, Ella couldn't help feeling shy and unsure. Yet she
wasn't a young girl anymore. She was an adult caught
up in something powerful and strong. She needed to
step back and look carefully before plunging in, despite what she was feeling.

"It's too soon," was all she could say, her voice
weak and fluttery in her throat.

"Stay," he urged her. "Please stay on Balboa with
me."

"I can't."

He kissed her again, softly. "Yes, you can," he insisted. "Just another day or two so we can get to know
each other better."

"I have commitments," she murmured.

"Can you break them?" he asked.

"I'd have to call the hospital."

"Hospital?"

"I volunteer twice a week at a hospital in Los Angeles," she told him.

"Can you find a substitute?"

"Oh, yes. There are lots of women who do volunteer work there, it's just that . . ."

"You're the best," he finished for her.

Ella laughed. "No, I'm not, really, but the children
seem to prefer me."

"I don't blame them. Their teacher is great fun," he
said, kissing her lightly on the corner of the mouth.
"Then you'll stay?"

Ella nodded and laughed again, almost nervously.
"I don't know what I'm getting myself into."

"Neither do I," Nick admitted, "but we'll find out together." Again he took her hand and they continued to walk along the beach silently, their bare feet splashing in the puddles created by the tide.

"What are you thinking?" he asked after a while.

"About your family."

Her answer surprised him. "My family? Why, for heaven's sake?"

"Because I'm a little intimidated by them. Generations of old Virginia traditions."

"Traditions aren't important, but people are. *You're* important, Ella. You're bright, inquisitive and imaginative, and that's what counts, not who you're related to."

"Even if your relatives are ambassadors and senators..."

"Even then," he said firmly, then added with a grin, "There's also a judge or two."

"I'm not surprised. And as for Nicholas Manning the Third, I guess you'll be an ambassador, too."

"I don't know," he said. "I haven't made any decisions about my future. Except to pursue you." He stopped walking and put his arm around her, hugging her close. "You will stay on, won't you?"

"For tomorrow anyway."

"Good. We'll take it a day at a time. Tomorrow we can sail to the small island across the lagoon."

"Won't that take a long time?"

"Yes," he said with a grin, "that's just the plan, all alone with you in a sailboat in the middle of the ocean."

* * *

When Ella returned to the bungalow, she wasn't surprised to find that Nikki was still awake, waiting to hear it all.

"I'll fix you a cup of coffee and you can tell me all about Nicholas Manning the Third, everything that you managed not to tell by running off to bed last night."

"Nikki, I don't want to drink coffee at this hour."

"Why not, for heaven's sake?"

"Because I'm getting up early in the morning, going sailing."

"Oh? And what about our ten o'clock plane?"

"I guess I'll have to miss it."

Nikki dropped back into the chair she'd just gotten out of. "You're staying over?"

Ella nodded.

"This *is* serious, just as I'd hoped."

"I'll have to get through to the hospital," Ella said, ignoring Nikki's comment.

"Don't worry about that. I'll take care of it. Now tell all."

"I like him, but we don't really know each other yet, and we thought that if I stayed for another day or two..."

"Or two?" The expression on Nikki's face showed absolute delight.

"We'll see what happens. There's so much we don't know about each other."

"He likes you; you like him. *I* like him. All the rest takes time."

Ella nodded, tried to meet Nikki's eye, then looked away, embarrassed. "I haven't told him."

"Told him what?"

Ella took a deep breath. "Who I am. Or rather who Cody is. He thinks I'm a woman named Ella Butler, born in Tyler, Texas, living in Los Angeles."

"He doesn't know you were Cody's wife?"

Ella shook her head.

"Where has this this guy been? Mars?" she asked incredulously.

"Almost. His most recent post was along the Pakistan–Afghanistan border. He's not the kind of man who's into show-business gossip, anyway. I expect he's heard of Cody, but he hasn't connected us."

"Very interesting," Nikki said. "So what are you going to do?"

"Tell him, of course. That's part of why I'm staying, part of our getting to know each other. It's going to be hard, though, because I've had such a wonderful time being myself. He likes me, Nikki. He thinks I'm special." Ella thought of their kiss in the moonlight and of his boast that he could climb the stairway to the moon beside her.

Nikki was pensive. "Sounds serious," she said finally. "Maybe Nick is the one whose genes are meant to mingle with yours." She grinned broadly, but the grin disappeared when she saw the expression on Ella's face.

"This isn't funny, Nikki."

"I see that it's not," Nikki said seriously. "I would say that you two are on the brink of falling in love. It certainly happened fast."

"Yes, it did. Too fast, maybe, for a man and a woman from such different backgrounds. His world isn't my world, Nikki."

"Any world is your world. You've traveled every-where." Nikki smiled. "Granted, you had to go out exploring the sights at night when there were no tour-ists around, but you explored them just the same, and during the day you wandered through all the out-of-the-way spots only the locals see. You're probably as knowledgeable about the world as anyone I know, in-cluding my darling Frank."

"Tell that to Nick's father, the ambassador. Can you imagine what he would think of me, the widow of a rock star?"

Nikki laughed. "I can only guess, but you'll never know until you give it a try. So go ahead and stay. Art will be a basket case, but I'll take care of him. You have yourself a wonderful time, and tell Nick the truth, Ella. Tell him about Cody."

"I will," Ella promised. "I was going to tell him tonight but—" she felt herself blush "—the moon-light got in my way."

The little sailboat heeled sharply in the wind, turned and raced toward shore through choppy waves. When the boat neared the beach, Nick jumped into the wa-ter and called out to Ella, "Lift up the centerboard, and I'll pull you in."

Ella did as directed, and when the boat's hull touched bottom, she was out in the water, too, pull-ing the tow line alongside Nick.

"We're a pretty good team, aren't we?" he asked when the boat was free of the water.

"You're certainly an understanding captain," Ella teased him, "to your crew of one."

"I'm trying to quell any chance of mutiny," he said, continuing in the spirit of fun that had been so much a part of their day. They'd sailed around the big island and then headed directly across the lagoon to the chain's smallest island, which was barely more than a half mile square of white beach and dense foliage. It was deserted now in the late afternoon as the new group of vacationers, some continuing their stay for another week, others just arriving, gathered back at Paradise Cove for cocktails.

"Does this island have a name?" Ella asked as they found a picnic spot under a palm tree at the edge of the beach.

"It's called Anca, and apparently it isn't a very popular spot. No signs that anyone's been here recently. Just the desert island I'd hoped we'd be stranded on."

"Except that we aren't stranded," Ella retorted as she unfolded the huge tablecloth the resort had supplied and spread it on the sand.

"That could be arranged. All I need is a high tide to come in and float the sailboat out to sea. Unfortunately, the tide's low, so I'll have to settle for a picnic on the beach."

"As planned," Ella said, "but which we won't have if you're going to leave the picnic hamper in the boat."

Nick shrugged and headed for the boat. Smiling, Ella watched him go. The interplay between them was so easy, as if they'd known each other forever. But mixed with it, adding another element to the relationship, was the feeling behind every look they exchanged, every accidental touch. Many times during

the day they'd been no more than a kiss apart. It was
a kiss that still waited for them.

Ella watched Nick reach into the boat for the hamper. He was stripped to the waist and wore a pair of
old sailing pants rolled up to his knees but still wet
from his plunge into the water. His back was sun-
burned from his sailing all day without a shirt, and
Ella expected that his skin would be hot to touch. She
could almost feel it burning beneath her fingertips,
and her blood tingled through her veins. As she
watched him turn and move toward her, the long
muscles in his arms rippling from the weight of the
picnic hamper, she felt a quick fluttering of her heart,
a sudden rush of adrenaline that left her both un-
nerved and excited.

"What is it, Ella?" he asked as he approached. He
must have noticed her staring. Embarrassed at having
been caught in such blatant admiration, Ella looked
away and anchored a corner of the tablecloth with a
large shell. "Nothing." She added, "The hamper
looks heavy."

"It is," he said, putting it down beside her. "This
is what the resort calls their 'lunch for two'; it's just
about enough for a small army."

"They must have seen us at the luau last night," she
said, and Nick joined in her laughter.

"Well, I'm not that hungry today."

"Neither am I," she answered, and for a long time
they just looked at each other, squinting in the fading
light of the sun, laughter on their lips. Ella felt at ease
with him and yet the tingling excitement remained
even when he looked away to open the hamper.

"What do you want to begin with?" he asked. He was kneeling beside her, pulling one item after another from the hamper. His hair fell in a dark comma over his forehead, and with a restless hand he brushed it back. "Hors d'oeuvres? Looks like some kind of pâté. Or how about deviled eggs?" Not waiting for her response, Nick continued to unload, setting the wrapped food before her. But Ella paid no attention to the food.

"Ella?" he asked when the hamper was finally empty. "Make a decision."

"I'm not really hungry." All she could think about was Nick beside her, the strong, firm muscles of his chest and back, shining with dampness from the sea. She took a deep breath and willed herself not to reach out and run her hand across his skin.

"Not even for chicken?" He extracted a drumstick from the wrapping.

She shook her head.

"Neither am I. We'll wait a while." As methodically as he'd unloaded, Nick began to put everything back in the hamper. When that was done, he turned to her and smiled. They were sitting very close, and his leg brushed against hers. Ella found herself nervously moving away, not because she didn't want to be near him but because being so close put her emotions in turmoil. That was evidently his intention, for Nick moved even closer, and the tingling in her veins intensified. All she could think of was last night, being in his arms, his mouth on hers.

"What is it, Ella?" he asked, reaching out to touch her face. "You seem so shy and yet there's so much understanding between us. Haven't you felt it all day?''

"Yes," she answered softly.

He tilted her chin and looked deeply into her eyes. His thumb moved back and forth across her chin, catching the lower edge of her lip, intruding once inside to the moist softness of her mouth. His eyes were dark and inquisitive, searching for an answer. "Last night I kissed you and you kissed me back, but even then I could sense your shyness. Are you unsure of your feelings for me?"

"No," she whispered. Her heart was pounding so loudly she knew he could hear it.

"Then what?" he persisted. His fingers still rested on her face; his hand cupped her chin.

"I suppose I'm unsure of myself."

Nick smiled, almost in disbelief. "I've never known anyone who had less reason to be unsure."

"I mean with you," she explained, knowing that she was making very little sense.

"Kiss me and tell me that again," he said, leaning toward her and brushing her lips gently. For a heartbeat, he hesitated, then, opening his mouth to speak her name, he covered her lips with his, drawing her into him, dizzying with intimacy.

When the kiss ended, Ella remained motionless, her eyes closed, and she heard him ask, "Are you still unsure?"

She shook her head, opened her eyes and looked into his. Now there seemed to be flecks of gold in his dark, dark eyes, but maybe it was just the light reflected from the setting sun.

"Then why are you frowning?" he asked gently.

Ella hadn't even known that she was frowning. "It's so difficult to explain," she said, shy again.

"Then let *me* explain something first." He settled her comfortably next to him and took her hand. "I didn't sleep very well last night; in fact, I hardly slept at all, thinking about you, wanting you. It's been a long time since anything in my life has felt this good. I know you're not the kind of woman to rush into anything, but I also know it feels right to you. I could tell from the beginning when we were exploring in Kikao and all day yesterday and again today. We're so right together, and I'm not even talking about the kiss, but that was right, too, more than anything. Wasn't it?"

"You keep asking me questions when you already know the answers." Her heart had slowed down a bit, but she was still very aware of him, his arm around her, the heat from his body melding into her own.

"But there's still something I don't know," he said softly.

"It's simple, really," she said, fighting the shyness that still held her. "I married very young. Before my husband, I'd never...been with a man. I haven't been with anyone since." She said the words and then leaned her head against his shoulder, her hair screening her face.

If her revelation surprised him, Nick didn't show it. He was still holding her hand. She could feel the pressure of his strong fingers covering hers. His silence encouraged her to go on.

"My life has been very strange, very protected. Contrary to what people might think, I'm not a worldly person." Ella knew that might confuse him, and she wondered if now was the time to tell him who she really was.

Suddenly that didn't seem necessary. He'd put his arms around her and was kissing her forehead, her eyes, her throat, kissing her softly and gently but with a passion that sent her reeling as if in an abyss. Reason was leaving her. Ella could feel it fleeing, and she knew that there would be no more words except the ones he was murmuring between kisses.

"I won't hurt you. I'd never hurt you, Ella. But this is so right for us. Nothing has ever been so right. Believe me."

She did believe him.

Chapter 4

In the treetops of Anca, exotic birds called out to one another; gentle waves rolled onto the white sand; a soft breeze stirred in the dense undergrowth. It was twilight. No other sounds disturbed the peace of the deserted island.

At the edge of the beach, the hamper that had been packed for their picnic was pushed aside, ignored. Ignored, too, was the tablecloth Ella had spread on the sand. She was lying on a big, fluffy beach towel, and Nick was by her side. For the first time in so very long she felt the touch of a strong male hand on her bare skin.

It was light, gentle, even careful, as his hand moved up her thigh. She was wearing shorts; Nick slipped his fingers beneath the fabric just an inch or two and all the while continued to kiss her, setting her on fire.

Still unsure of her reaction to his touch and to his
kiss, Nick had checked his own urges, willing himself
to go slowly. It wouldn't be easy, because inside his
passions were raging, screaming to be set free. Yet he
knew Ella's fears, and he was willing to wait for a sign
from her.

It came very soon, in an even deeper response than
when he'd kissed her on the beach. He felt her give
herself over to it, melting against him and into him,
returning with equal urgency the fervor of his hungry
mouth. That's when he moved his hand to touch her
round firm breast. He heard a sound escape her lips
between their kisses, and he drew his hand away,
wondering if he'd gone too far, too fast.

Then he had the answer to every silent question
about her feelings for him and what was to come. She
reached out and caught his hand in hers and returned
it to her body, opening the front of her shirt so that he
could cup her bare breast.

That first touch would be forever sealed in his mind,
the sensuality in her gesture as much as—no, *more*
than, he thought wildly—the actual sensation he felt
when his hand held her. One thing he knew; from this
moment, they were one as much as if they were actually joined.

They struggled together to free Ella of her cotton
shirt and the flimsy wisp of a bra beneath it, and then
he held her close, her naked breasts against his bare
chest. He caressed her back and shoulders and felt her
fingers digging into him, pulling him closer and closer
as he kissed her all over, her eyes, her mouth, her neck
and downward. His lips burned a damp trail to her
breast, and when he caught her nipple in his mouth,

he heard her say, "Yes, yes," in a voice that was thick with need.

Ella now knew that all her doubts about him and herself were unfounded. A sigh of relief swept through her, and she joined him in an almost frantic removal of the rest of their clothes. They actually laughed together for a moment as they tried to free him of his trousers, which were still wet from his jump into the water. Finally, he kicked them off, rolled over and held her in his arms until she was on top of him and they were melded together along every inch of their bodies.

The rest was so natural that it seemed as if they'd always been lovers, each knowing what the other felt, each anticipating the other's needs. Turning again, they were side by side, opening their eyes to gaze deeply, moving their hands to caress secret places expectantly.

Ella touched him with wonder and yet without great surprise. Holding him was instinctive; it seemed so right. And when she felt his hand move across her hipbone and down her abdomen, she opened for him, letting his fingers find that eager, sweet place that was honeyed with desire.

Her need was so intense that when he touched her, every fiber of Ella's being thrilled to that touch. She wondered if she would die from the pleasure, the spiraling passion that made her reach out for him with her heart and soul and body.

"This is what I've wanted for so long, Ella, and now I know that it's time." Nick's voice was hoarse, as if he could barely get out the words.

"Yes," she whispered, "it's time for us."

He rose above her, and she lifted her hips to meet him and welcome him inside, and in that instant when they became truly one, the whole island seemed to be their own special world where the birds sang and the waves rippled and the breeze rustled the trees, all because of the two lovers there on the beach, for them alone.

The moment wasn't over then; it was only beginning. He seemed to grow in her and for her until Ella was brought to the brink of ecstasy, and then he drew out and then plunged even deeper, again and again. She moved with him until he could hold back no longer. Nick looked into her eyes and saw the answer there and felt it in her body, which arched upward to meet each thrust, fiercer now, much fiercer. The great spasm that followed seemed to go on and on until they cried out together with voices from the depth of their passion.

It was a long time before Ella heard the sounds of the island again. They returned one at a time into her awareness, first the birds and then the waves and finally the breeze. She opened her eyes and looked around. It was almost dark; the white sand glowed pinkly all around them.

"Nick..."

"Yes?" He'd been waiting for her to speak but realized he'd have to wait a little longer, because she couldn't seem to find any more words. "What is it, Ella?"

"You were right," she whispered.

"I know, I know." He hugged her close.

For now, they didn't need to say any more. They understood each other and the completeness of what had happened between them. No questions needed to be asked; no explanations given. There was peace and satisfaction everywhere, even in the air around them.

After a while they stirred, roused themselves and ate their picnic, talking and laughing until far into the night. Then they sailed home in the dark with the beam on their sailboat directing them across the glassy smooth lagoon.

They passed the night in Nick's bungalow, sleeping in each other's arms, waking, making love and falling back into a deep sleep, wrapped together comfortably.

"Will you stay another day?" he asked sometime during the night, and she answered that she would. She'd never had any doubt.

"Two?" he asked, and she laughed, not answering. Sometime, she knew, it would have to end and Ella would have to go back to being Cody Butler's widow. But she didn't say that; she couldn't. Not yet, not while life was being returned to her in such abundance.

They went shopping that morning along the row of resort stores. In one she bought fabric to have dresses made in the native style for herself, Nikki and Susan.

"Do you sew?" he asked her casually.

"No, but I have a dressmaker," Ella answered without even realizing until later that the world in which she lived was beginning to show.

She had trouble making up her mind among the many different patterns, but the shopkeeper had an answer for that. "The madam should take them all," he suggested.

"Maybe I will," Ella said, then began to barter. Nick had convinced her that the merchants had a price in mind and part of the challenge for them was bargaining with the customers until that price was reached.

He watched with a half smile on his face, delighting in her mixture of sophistication and innocence. For three days he'd enjoyed her ability to get happiness from the simplest things. She was more than his fantasy come to life; she was an answer to a prayer. He'd begun to think about spending the rest of his life with her.

Nick watched as she went into the back of the shop, carrying her bolts of cloth to have the material cut. When she disappeared through the curtain he felt a pang in his heart; he didn't like to have her out of his sight. Nick shook his head in wonder. This was all so new to him. He was falling in love.

He was just about to go into the back after her when Ella reappeared. She looked, he thought, more beautiful than ever. But he'd thought that often since the first time he'd seen her. He reached out and took her arm, and just touching her brought back the recent memories of their night together.

"I think it's time for me to cool off," he said with a grin.

She looked at him with a puzzled expression, but when she saw the glimmer in his eyes, he didn't need to explain.

"Maybe we should go for a swim," she suggested.

"A good plan. Grab a bathing suit, and I'll meet you at the beach."

That was how their morning progressed, spontaneously, interrupted by pauses to touch and kiss and hold each other before moving on to the next unplanned activity, which, after their swim, was a try at sailboarding. It was a sport neither of them had ever attempted and at which they were both miserable failures. Another three days of lessons, the instructor told them, and they'd be able to keep the Windsurfer upright, but even Nick knew that they didn't have three more days.

After lunch they took the motor launch to Kikao, where they'd decided to spend the night. There were huts for rent in a coconut grove near the beach, one of the brochures informed them, and although they didn't remember seeing any signs of life in the grove, they decided to take a chance.

"They're a little primitive," Nick said when they stepped inside one of the huts, led by the proprietor, who was also owner of the restaurant.

"Running water," he proudly told his guests.

"Cold only," Nick added to Ella.

"In this heat, a cold shower sounds fine," Ella responded, trying not to think about the lack of pressure in the pitiful little shower head.

"The hut's not air-conditioned," Nick went on, listing his second complaint.

"No, but we'll get a nice breeze," Ella reminded him, and he knew that was so because the hut's walls were made of woven coconut fronds, the roof thatched with coconut leaves.

Ella had an answer for all his objections, and as he paid for the night in advance and sent the proprietor off, Nick laughed with joy. "I was hoping you'd like it."

"Then why did you complain so much?" she asked.

He put his arm around her and kissed the top of her head. "So you'd have a chance to back out if you wanted to."

"Never," she said. "It's paradise."

Again he saw the Ella that he'd suddenly fallen in love with, an adventurous woman who could find joy anywhere. Before they went out to explore he took the time to tell Ella what she was beginning to mean to him, and he tried not to worry that her responsiveness had a touch of foreboding, if not sadness, in it.

Their exploring took them past the village along a narrow, dusty road. As they walked, Ella began to get a better idea of the life of the Kikaoans who lived outside the village among the natural resources of the island, groves of coconut, papaya and banana trees. These fruits and the fish they caught seemed to make up the Kikaoans' diet as well as their livelihood, for they sold what they didn't consume at the market on the big island.

Nick had been right when they'd visited there before; tourism assured survival and yet the ways of these people living on the periphery of tourism were still primitive.

The island, like all the others in the chain, had once been under the rule of the British, who'd brought their religion and their language; otherwise, there was very little that was English here.

"This seems like a life from centuries ago," Ella observed, watching the women at work weaving baskets and stringing beads.

"It is," Nick agreed. "As they grow up, some of the children probably will leave to find work in Australia or New Zealand, but those who have stayed lead a simple life."

Further along, near a primitive hut, two men squatted in the dirt, mending a double canoe. The adults smiled and went on with their work, paying little heed to the intruders, but the children were more friendly—and more sales-oriented. Ella found herself buying again, strings of beads and baskets in different shapes. In fact, she liked the baskets so much that she was soon loaded down with them, and Nick had some difficulty getting her away and back toward the village.

"I've never seen such fine work," Ella remarked as he ushered her off. "Look at the weave, Nick."

He laughed. "It is intricate, but a person can own just so many baskets," he insisted.

"True, but a person can give them away." As she spoke, Nick managed to maneuver her away from the young salesmen and on the way back down the road. But there was still a stop Ella wanted to make.

As quaint as the island ways seemed, there was always potential, here as anywhere in the world, for illness and injury, and she was now aware that the population of the island was far greater than she'd first thought. In those hills they hadn't had time to explore was another village and, looming over it, a villa built by a wealthy Englishman and deserted long ago. Except for Balboa, Kikao was the largest island in the chain. Yet the doctor visited infrequently.

"Let's go by that courtyard at the end of the street," Ella suggested suddenly.

"You want to see the clinic again, don't you?"

"Maybe the doctor's there today," she answered.

He wasn't. The low building was still closed up tightly, but a small group of Kikaoans was gathered on the steps.

Ella approached and asked again, as she had before, when the doctor would arrive.

"Maybe today," a woman holding a child in her lap answered.

Ella mused that time didn't seem to have much meaning for them; they were prepared to wait. "Nick..."

"Neither of us is qualified to help these people, Ella. When we get back to Balboa we'll find out when the doctor *is* coming."

"*If* he's coming," Ella said a little bitterly.

"I'm sure he'll get here soon," Nick assured her, "but in the meantime, there's nothing we can do."

Ella was thoughtful, then finally said, as much to herself as to him, "There's something I can do."

"I know you volunteer at the hospital, but do you think you have enough medical background—"

"No," Ella said. "Certainly not, but there are other ways I can help."

"It's not always so simple." The diplomat in Nick wanted to explain about the suffering he'd seen throughout the world, suffering brought on as much by man's inhumanity to man as by disease, as much by wars as by plagues. Many times he'd seen situations in which the purchase of food would save a starving people, but the food never reached them because of politics, the dissension among governments.

"It's very complicated, Ella," he told her, "this subject of suffering."

"But *this* isn't complicated. All that's needed here is an endowment to upgrade the clinic and bring in a permanent medical team. I think I can help."

"Can you afford that, Ella?"

"Yes," she said simply.

When she didn't amplify on her answer, Nick asked no questions. He sensed that when she was ready, she would tell him about herself. For now he knew only that Ella Butler was a wealthy woman, and somehow he'd known that all along. The surprise was in her lifestyle here with him, in her innocence and joy, her unspoiled nature.

They took their time going back, stopping again and again to watch the Kikaoans at work and at play. Most of the women were quite plump and the men as thin as reeds; all of them exchanged greetings with Nick and Ella without being overly friendly. However, the children were full of enthusiasm over the two strangers among them. Ella chatted with them all and bought more of their goods while Nick watched, smiling.

Her mood had lifted, and she felt like a tourist again, enjoying the island with Nick, reveling in that spirit of freedom that had for days allowed her to be herself, wishing this time together could go on and on. Occasionally she'd been able to give way to the hope that it could, knowing but not allowing herself to admit that such a hope was groundless. Something always seemed to happen that brought her back to reality.

Today it was more than just a reminder that insinuated itself into the fun. It was Cody himself, in the most unlikely place. One of his old songs blared over the radio at the little store where they stopped for a cold drink. It was a scratchy but very recognizable old hit song. Ella glanced quickly at Nick, who was engrossed in examining the store's wares and didn't seem to hear the music, but it had brought Ella back to reality with a jolt. She felt certain that a flush had spread for an instant over her face. She finally controlled it and hoped he hadn't noticed.

Nick *had* noticed; he noticed everything about her. Even when he wasn't looking at her directly, he was so aware of her that he picked up all the vibes. "Is everything okay?" he asked, reaching for her hand.

Ella smiled, erasing whatever expression lingered on her face. "Fine," she said as she finished her drink. "It's probably just the heat."

"It'll be much cooler in our room," he suggested. "Remember? We get a nice breeze," he quoted Ella's earlier observation. "Especially now, with the long shadows from the trees." He'd begun to think about the hut, a little primitive but not lacking in charm, nestled there in the coconut grove at the edge of the beach. The bed had been big and comfortable-looking; he'd noticed that immediately. In fact, it had been all he could do to keep from taking her to bed right there and then. She'd wanted to explore, though, so he'd gone with her and enjoyed himself thoroughly in her company. Now it was time to take her home, for he felt that it would be home for them, there by the sea. But then, he mused, any place would feel like home with Ella.

"Are you ready to go back now?" he asked without being able to keep the huskiness of desire from his voice.

"Yes," she answered softly. The look on her face now was the look he'd hoped to see there. It was sweetness mixed with desire, and he'd never known a look to compare with it.

The early-evening sun had faded away almost completely, but what faint rays remained filtered in through the thatched roof and spread out in soft yellow strips across the naked bodies lying side by side on the cotton-covered mattress. Ella's eyes were closed, but he knew that she wasn't asleep because of the little smile that flickered on her face. He stroked her soft hair, which was still damp from their lovemaking, and wiped away the little trickle of perspiration on her forehead. It was cool in the hut, but even an arctic breeze couldn't have cooled the heat of their passion. It had been so complete that Nick had wondered for a long moment afterward where his body ended and hers began.

Lackadaisically, he let his hand drift down her shoulder to her upper arm, across her breast, lingering there before he slid it on along her body. Ella's smile widened, and then as he tickled the inside of her thigh she giggled and opened her eyes.

"I can't keep my hands off you," he murmured. "I'm like a kid who's just taken the top off the cookie jar and reached inside. There's so much good to choose from. All so tasty." He nibbled on her shoulder.

She snuggled up close to him and kissed his mouth lightly, running her tongue along his bottom lip. "You're pretty delicious yourself."

He returned the kiss and felt a stirring deep inside. So soon, he was overcome by her again. Nick had to force himself to end the kiss. There was something he needed to say, but he was having trouble finding the words. Nick Manning, who'd faced guerrilla leaders, heads of state, men and women of power all over the world, was suddenly speechless. He'd handled so many tough situations with finesse, but he couldn't find the words to tell this delicate woman what he felt, that he was in love with her.

"We need to make plans," he began weakly.

"For dinner?" she asked, nuzzling his shoulder.

Well, Nick thought, he'd mishandled that completely. Might as well just come right out and say it. "For the future."

He watched as she opened her eyes wide and then frowned a little. He'd gone from subtlety to bluntness that shocked. Fool, he decided, just step on in.

"For when we get back to the States. When we get home." He waited, not about to look at her face again for fear he'd see another frown there.

"I want to see you when we get back, Ella, spend more time with you. This isn't a holiday fling we're on. We both know that." There. He didn't know any other way to say it except to tell her that he loved her, and she wasn't ready to hear that yet. He knew that much.

Ella only knew the time had come. This was it, she thought. Now she had to tell him about Cody. She'd known it would have to happen, but it seemed so quick. She just wasn't ready. She wanted more time to be Ella with him, to be free and easy and loving. She didn't want it to end!

When she didn't answer, Nick pressed her. "What is it, Ella? Don't you want to see me again when we get back?"

"Of course I do. It's just that . . ."

"It's time for an answer, Ella. Either *yes* or *no*."

He wasn't hesitant now; he was taking control, she noted. There was a sharp, commanding edge to his voice. She realized that he was a man used to getting what he wanted, at least used to getting answers.

"My answer isn't *no*, Nick, but yours might be when you hear about me."

Nick looked her in the eye, probing and unrelenting. "I can't think of anything you can tell me that would make my answer *no*. I know you aren't married, and I know you aren't involved in a serious relationship. Nothing else matters. You could be an underworld princess or even a real princess. You could be a hardened criminal, although I must say I have trouble visualizing that one. You could be—"

"That's enough, Nick." Moving away from him, she got out of bed, pulled on her shorts and shirt and went out the door of their hut, through the trees and onto the beach. It was dark, and the moon was just beginning to light the sky and accent the whitecaps far out at sea. She had only a few seconds to take everything in and draw a deep breath to prepare herself before Nick was beside her.

He reached out and took her arm, looking deeply into her eyes. "You're not joking, are you?"

"No."

"This is something serious."

"Yes." She couldn't muster more than one-word answers.

"Then for God's sake tell me, Ella. Who are you?"

"It's not who I am; it's who I was." She took a deep breath. "I was Cody Butler's wife."

There was a split second of silence before Nick let out a low whistle. "I'll be damned. Ella *Butler*. I never put it together. I guess I'm not much of a celebrity follower."

Ella managed to laugh. "No, I can see that."

"But I certainly know that Cody was—"

"Famous? Flamboyant? Powerful?"

This time Nick laughed. He was interested but no longer wary. While the news was certainly a surprise to him, it wasn't at all threatening. "I suppose he was all of those things, at least from what I can remember of his mystique. But why didn't you tell me this, Ella?"

"There are so many reasons," Ella answered. She walked a little away from him, onto the edge of the sand, and Nick stood still, watching her in the moonlight, waiting. "I came here to get away from myself, away from being Cody's widow. But even at Paradise Cove it took me a while to realize that I could be *me*. Nikki had to give me a big push. Then I found out that no one here cared what I wore or who I had dinner with. It was such a relief, Nick."

Nick was still puzzled. "Your husband died more than two years ago. Don't tell me you're still hounded by fans."

"Oh, Nick," she said with a sigh. "You *don't* understand. That's why it was so wonderful being with you. You saw me just as Ella; you knew me that way."

"I still do. That hasn't changed just because I now know who your husband was. It can't matter in the least."

"It matters. This isn't the real world for me. My world is very reclusive. I can't go shopping or out to dinner or to a movie without reporters and fans following me, hanging on to me."

"Good Lord," Nick said. "I had no idea."

She continued. "There's a strange mystique surrounding Cody even in death. Yes, it's been more than two years, but to his fans it was only yesterday. They probably would have been happy if I'd thrown myself on a funeral pyre. The only good I serve is to keep his flame alive."

"That's terrible." Nick's distress showed as he moved to where Ella stood and put his arm around her. "Break away, Ella, and live your own life. You've proven here with me during these last few days that it's possible."

She shook her head sadly. "The real world isn't the same."

"I can handle the real world, Ella. I'm not at all worried about it. Just so we can be together." He held her closer and caressed her hair, watching the moonlight dance on it, forgetting all about what she'd told him. For him, Ella had no connection with Cody Butler.

Ella didn't relax in his arms, and when she looked up at him her eyes seemed terribly sad.

"Ella—"

"Oh, Nick, what you want isn't possible. Our worlds are too different."

"It doesn't matter," he reiterated.

"It will matter. Every time we go out reporters will appear to ask you all kinds of personal questions, questions that are no one's business." Ella spoke adamantly.

"Which is exactly what I'll tell them," Nick answered just as adamantly.

"They'll compare you to Cody, and they'll bring up the past," she warned.

"I'm Nicholas Manning," he said, speaking the words very clearly and with total confidence. "I won't be compared to anyone, Ella."

"I know that, Nick, but it won't keep them from trying, from bringing up my past."

"The past doesn't matter." He held her tightly. "It's over."

"It's there," she insisted, "recorded on film and in still photographs."

"They're only pictures, Ella."

"Wait until you see them. Me with my hair bleached platinum blond, in a skintight silver lamé jumpsuit. That's how I dressed for Cody; that's how I looked. It would really impress your bosses at the State Department."

Nick smiled to himself, kissed her cheek and told her, "I'm a big boy, Ella. I can handle it."

Ella wouldn't be denied. "What about your family? I can't imagine they'll want to clip your pictures from the scandal sheets and add them to the Manning photo album."

Nick had to laugh when he thought about that. "This isn't about my family, though. It's about me and you and our feelings for each other. Let me tell you about *my* feelings, Ella." He turned her in his

arms and looked down at her with all the tenderness
he possessed. "I'm falling in love with you. No, don't
turn away." He placed the palm of his hand against
her cheek and kept her face steady, directly in his gaze.
"I love you, and I don't want this to end when we
leave here. I won't let it end."

"You might not be able to control what happens,
Nick."

"Trust me. You can trust me, can't you, Ella?"

"Yes."

"Good. That's important, but it doesn't even matter unless you feel the same way I feel. Do you, Ella?"

"Yes, Nick," she whispered, "I do."

Hearing those words, Nick dropped his defenses.
All of the power drained from him. He was hers completely. He kissed her passionately, and she clung to
him. That contact was all he needed. The flame was
rekindled. He leaned over, picked her up and carried
her back to the hut. "We'll be together," he told her,
"not just now, but when we go home."

Nick was more than true to his word. He didn't wait
until they returned to the States to see Ella again; he
insisted on going back with her and stopping at La
Casa before returning to Washington. Ella, unwilling
for him to be caught in the trap of her celebrity right
away, begged Nick to let her make the arrangements.
He knew that she was apprehensive, so he agreed.

They returned on the Butler private plane, arrived
at the airport late at night and drove to the house before dawn—and the crowds—descended on La Casa.

Chapter 5

Nick had adopted kind of an amused attitude toward arrangements for their trip to Los Angeles. All the precautions seemed just a little ridiculous to a man who'd been involved in life-or-death situations abroad. It had often been necessary for him to drive to and from embassies and other American facilities in bulletproof cars with armed guards. In times of crisis he'd dodged not only reporters but militants, terrorists and aggressors of every sort. For Ella Butler to be so cautious in simply returning to her home in California struck him as ludicrous, but because she was so adamant he didn't protest.

"I want us to have a pleasant return," she'd told him. "It would be easier and certainly more natural for us to meet somewhere away from Los Angeles."

"No," he'd insisted. "I want to see what your life as Ella Butler is all about."

"Then I must plan carefully, Nick, or we'll attract a swarm of reporters. Believe me."

"I'll bow to your wisdom," he said, giving her a kiss but retaining his skepticism over the necessity for all her precautions.

That skepticism lasted until they reached the top of Laurel Canyon high above Los Angeles and he saw the fans waiting at the La Casa gates.

"It's not even six in the morning," he said, amazed.

"Some of them hang around all night" was Ella's response as the chauffeur sped up, passed the house and turned onto the back road.

"What are they waiting for?" Nick asked as he looked over his shoulder at the determined group of fans.

"Me," Ella answered simply. "I'm all that's left for them of Cody, and they've made this Cody's shrine. I go through the front gate often when I have time, stop and talk with them for a few minutes, sign some autographs. That's all they want. They're not disrespectful."

"But what a nuisance," Nick observed.

Ella just smiled. He was about to be initiated into the trials and tribulations of being involved with Ella Butler. She hoped he could survive.

She showed him the house with some trepidation, thinking of who Nick was, where he came from, the genteel life in the peaceful countryside of Virginia. She imagined the Manning home was tastefully decorated, showing not the slightest sign of ostentation in its fine antiques passed down from generation to generation. There were antiques at La Casa, but they certainly had no connection to Ella's family or to Cody's.

Some of the rooms, Ella had to admit, were a little less than subtle in their decor.

Nick stopped for a long while to study the larger-than-life portrait of Cody that dominated the entrance hall; then he made the rest of the tour quietly, observing but not commenting as they moved from room to room until they reached Ella's office. It was her haven; it was all Ella, and he seemed to respond to that immediately.

"So you spend a lot of time here?" he asked as they relaxed on the bright chaise.

"Just about all my waking hours. I even sleep here occasionally. That sofa against the wall makes into a bed."

"The room is delightful, Ella, just the kind of setting I'd pictured you in."

Ella smiled knowingly. "But you hadn't pictured me in the rest of Cody's house."

"Cody's house?"

"I guess that's the way I still think of La Casa. It was never really my house, or my life, for that matter. I was just a part of what was his."

Nick frowned deeply, and she tried to explain. "My life with Cody was very unusual. I've tried to tell you that."

"Yes, you have. Now I'd like to hear it all, and afterward I'd like to put it behind us, Ella. Because it *is* over, you know."

She didn't answer, wondering if it would ever really be over.

"Now tell me," he said, taking her hand, "how a little gal from somewhere near Tyler, Texas, ended up in this place called La Casa."

Ella leaned back on the chaise, answering somewhat ruefully, "I often wonder the same thing. I was barely eighteen when Cody gave a concert in Dallas. Somehow the Chamber of Commerce of Tyler convinced his public relations people to bring Cody to town to judge a beauty contest. If it hadn't been early in his career, he wouldn't have done it, but in those days he relished the publicity."

"You were in the beauty contest," Nick guessed.

"Yes."

"And of course you won."

"Yes, and Cody put the crown on my head. I was mesmerized by him. It was that simple."

Nick watched her without response.

"Nothing was ever simple again," Ella continued. "He wanted me to fly to Los Angeles the next week to visit him. My parents were horrified, of course, so Cody sent them tickets, too. We came to L.A. and spent a week in his home. That was before he built La Casa. My parents returned to Texas; I stayed. It seemed like a miracle that Cody Butler would love me and marry me."

Nick didn't think that sounded like a miracle at all. "And you loved him." He made it a statement, rather than a question. Nevertheless, he waited for the answer.

"I was caught up in the aura of Cody Butler, and I'm sure I thought that was love. It was certainly all I'd ever known of love, and it became my life." She thought about this for a long moment. "I was swept off my feet by the strength of my feelings for him. I suppose I never really got over that, even at the end." She didn't want to tell Nick about the last years, when their lives had begun to fall apart. "There was a sort of magic about him," she said evasively, "not just for me but for everyone who ever knew him or even saw him perform. That never really faded. And, yes, for me it took the form of love."

"I didn't expect to hear otherwise," Nick admitted, "but it makes me jealous just the same." He shook his head in wonder. "I haven't been jealous in a long time. I suppose I haven't cared about anyone enough." He looked at her long and hard. There was something else he had to know, and he knew he would be able to see it in her eyes. "How do you feel about him now?"

She returned his gaze steadily. "It's hard to describe my feelings; they're so mixed." She was thoughtful. "I've never tried to put them into words."

"Do you still love him?"

"No," she said quietly but emphatically. "I don't still love him. I can sit here now, in his house, and tell you that."

His house. Nick didn't comment on her use of words. "But you aren't so eager to be caught up in those kinds of feelings again." He was thinking of *them* now, of himself and Ella. He'd been thinking of them all along.

"I'm a very different person from that girl who entered the beauty contest in Texas. I've had a lot of catching up to do in the last two years, a lot of growing up. I'm not there yet," she admitted, "but I'm trying."

Nick reached out and took her in his arms. "That's what I want, Ella, for you to keep growing but just to save some room in your life for me."

Ella held on to him almost fiercely. She wanted what Nick wanted. They'd shared so much in the few days they'd been together, and the future he envisioned sounded so perfect. It was just possible that it could all happen.

"That's what I want, too, for us to have room in our lives for each other." Even as she spoke, Ella couldn't contain the apprehension that forced her to wonder if it could ever be.

His words showed no such doubt. "I'll see that we have it," he said confidently, "but as for the present, it's 8:00 a.m., and I'm beginning to feel the jet lag. How about you?"

"Mmm," Ella said softly against his shoulder.

"Then let's go to bed," he said without hiding the insinuation in his voice.

"Mmm," she sighed again, but roused herself quickly. "I'd better let everyone know."

"That we're going to bed?" Nick's perplexity was immediate.

Ella laughed. "We don't want the normal routine to get going all around us. Juanita usually wakes me about this time. We go over the day's menus, after breakfast I meet with the staff and—"

"Wait. Hold everything," he said, interrupting her. "Let's go back to that first one. Juanita wakes you up. Don't you have a clock, Ella?"

Ella laughed. "Of course, but that's the routine, the way it's always been."

He raised a quizzical eyebrow.

"All right," Ella said with another laugh, "it won't be that way today. But..." She paused, waiting for a response.

"Go ahead; I'm prepared."

"I do need to look through my messages. I can see the stack Nikki left on my desk. It's pretty high, Nick."

He helped her up from the chaise. "Go ahead. I'll make myself scarce."

"No," she said, holding on to his hand. "Stay here. I'll just take care of the ones that sound urgent."

Ella sat down at the desk and Nick perched on the corner next to her, interested, curious and then fascinated as she handled the messages, dictated responses to letters, returned calls to the East Coast and then attacked a second pile of memos on the desk.

"Who's that from?" Nick asked casually.

"Art Newcombe."

"I thought Nikki was your secretary."

"She is, and Art is Cody's manager." Ella was reading through a long note, frowning, checking her calendar as she talked. "I see he's accepted invitations for me and set up interviews that I didn't know anything about until now. Sometimes I could—"

"Ella." Nick stopped her again in midsentence. He was trying to get it all straight. "I can understand that everything goes on here at the house as it did before your husband died, but there's something that doesn't make any sense to me at all. Maybe it's none of my business. Maybe I'm jumping in where I'm not wanted, prying too much."

"No, Nick, you're not prying. You wanted to see my life, and you were right." She gestured to the crowded desk top. "This is part of it. I know it seems an odd way for me to spend my time, but I've been left with certain obligations. I've tried to phase them out one by one without cutting myself off completely. There are so many organizations that Cody supported, and I want to remain involved with most of them, if not personally, then by donations.''

"I understand that, Ella. But let me ask my question. Why this Newcombe fellow? What is there to manage?''

Ella leaned back in her desk chair, closed the calendar and put down her pen. "The estate has become a vast enterprise. Arthur handles everything that relates to Cody, from the rerelease of records, movies on tape, cable programs, to my participation in functions that commemorate Cody or lend his name to products.''

"And for this he gets his ten percent?''

"Fifteen, actually,'' Ella said. "He's a manager, not an agent.''

"I see. I don't suppose he manages anyone else?''

"No,'' Ella responded. "This takes all of his time. As I told you, I'm trying to phase some of it out, but a few things will have to remain active, and I need Art to manage them for me. But all these appearances are ridiculous, and I'm going to put a stop to them.'' She looked up at Nick. "That's part of the way I'm changing, Nick.''

"That's my girl.''

"For instance,'' she continued, "I'm not going to the opening of a new theater in the San Fernando Valley even if it is named for Cody. Instead—'' she looked at him teasingly ''—I'm going to get over my jet lag.''

"And that could take all morning,'' Nick told her with a glint in his eye.

"Don't underestimate us," Ella said a little more boldly than she would have expected of herself. "It could take all afternoon."

"I sincerely hope so" was Nick's response.

Ella took his hand and led him into the hall. They paused at double doors, which were ornately carved in dark mahogany. Ella reached for the brass knob, found it and hesitated. "This is my room . . . the one I shared with Cody."

Nick saw the look of confusion on her face. "I'm sure there are lots of rooms in La Casa," he answered easily. "I think we'd be more comfortable in another one, *our* room."

The relief on her face was evident as she led him to an open door at the end of the hall. The furniture in the bedroom was Spanish, heavily carved, dark and almost overpowering. Ella moved across the plush wine-colored carpet and closed the damask draperies. Like all of La Casa, except for her office, the room was overdone and almost claustrophobic. It was more than ever Cody's house, Nick reflected.

As she turned back toward him, Nick read the indecision in her eyes. He moved to her and took her in his arms. "This is tough on you, isn't it, bringing another man into Cody's domain?"

She looked at him, trying to put her mixed emotions into words. "I want you here, Nick. I want to be with you more than anything. It seemed so right on Balboa . . ."

"But it doesn't seem the same here," he finished for her. "Right man, wrong place." He tried to joke even though his heart felt leaden and heavy.

"It can be the same again; I'm sure of that." Ella spoke vehemently as if to convince both herself and Nick.

"Then we'll wait," he said with more equanimity than he felt. "We're both tired out from the flight. I can sleep here, and you can go to your room. Or," he suggested, trying to keep his voice casual, "we can both stretch out here."

"I feel as though I've let you down," she said quietly.

He tilted her face and looked into her deep blue eyes, which were so guileless and sincere. With any other woman he might have thought the sudden skittishness a game-playing tactic to gain the upper hand in their budding relationship, but not with Ella. He'd promised not to push her; he certainly wasn't going to do so now.

"Listen to me, Ella Butler. There's more to being with you than making love. That's a wonderful part of what makes us special, but not all of it." He kissed her, then sat down to pull off his shoes. "Let's get some sleep, Ella. We have the rest of the day—and the night."

Ella woke late, as they'd both expected, knowing that nothing in her life had ever compared to the bond of understanding that she shared with Nick. It promised to be greater than any obstacle set in its way, and Ella knew there would be many; she'd already faced some of them during their first morning at La Casa. Nick had yet to confront the others that caused barriers between Ella and the outside world. She hoped he would never have to see crowds reaching for her, reporters pushing their mikes in her face, but she was afraid nothing could prevent it. Nick evidently felt otherwise. He clearly had something on his mind. As they climbed out of bed and into swimsuits for a dip in the pool before their late lunch, he was full of questions followed by suggestions.

"Which of Cody's projects are you dedicated to?"

"Just the hospital, really, helping children," she answered.

"The others could survive with only your financial help?"

"Yes," she said, pulling two towels from the linen closet before they headed downstairs.

"Nikki can handle most of your correspondence?" He took her hand as they walked down the staircase to the foyer.

"Easily," Ella admitted.

"Is that what you foresee for the future, easing out of your life as Cody's widow?"

"I've already begun to, but I can't desert everything at once. It takes time."

He didn't remind her that two years had passed. He wanted to set the stage for the future, not dictate it. As they crossed the foyer to the back patio, Juanita passed, greeting them cheerfully, and Nick thought he detected a sparkle of approval in her eye. Not so with the gardener, he definitely had a scornful look for the intruder. Not all of the staff would easily adjust to having another man at La Casa.

Nick and Ella dived into the pool and swam half a dozen laps. Then they stopped and hung on to the side of the pool at the deep end, laughing at their breathlessness. "Scuba diving didn't take this kind of energy," Nick said. "Is this how you keep in shape?"

"It *was*," Ella answered with a grin as she pushed the strands of wet hair away from her face. "I'm going to have to ease my way back into the regime."

"Well, whatever you're doing, keep it up. I approve of the results."

"Why, thank you, Mr. Manning," she said, kissing him wetly on the mouth. It felt good to be so free and easy with him. Ella suspected that somewhere Joe, the gardener, was watching, and disapproving, but she didn't care. Her life was going to change.

They dried off and stretched out beside the pool to eat the late lunch Juanita had prepared for them while she stood nearby, chatting with Nick in Spanish. Ella was impressed. "I guess I imagined you spoke French, since it's the language of diplomacy, but I didn't know you'd been posted to any Spanish-speaking countries."

"Actually, I haven't, but I picked up the language somewhere along the way. I don't think facility with language has anything to do with brains—"

"I hope not," Ella laughed, "because after all these years with Juanita, I still have a vocabulary of about a hundred words."

"It's a knack, that's all. Seems to run in my family."

"How many languages do you speak?"

"Let's see." He thought a moment. "Five, and then a few African dialects."

"A true diplomat," Ella said, then added thoughtfully, "It must be a fascinating life."

"At times. It can be monotonous; it can also be dangerous. And sometimes very lonely."

As they lingered over their lunch, Nick reminisced about some of the countries he'd lived in during his career. Ella listened with fascination until long after Juanita had cleared away the dishes, the gardeners had put up their tools and the late-afternoon sun had shifted in the sky to leave them in cool shade.

They'd moved around, changing positions until Ella was stretched out beside the pool, dangling one hand in the water and Nick was sitting beside her, his feet submerged. He ran his hand along her damp brown leg, and Ella felt the little tremor of excitement she suspected would always accompany his touch, for there was between them that instant attraction that had begun one day on a launch crossing the bay to Kikao. Nothing could endanger it except, Ella thought, her life and all the complications that went with it. A noise from outside brought them back vividly.

"What's that?" Nick asked.

The sound had intensified; it was music, one of Cody's songs that Nick wouldn't have recognized, being sung by a very mixed group of fans.

"Sometimes they have impromptu concerts," Ella told him. She was used to the activity that took place outside La Casa, but Nick was amazed by it.

"Why don't you move, Ella? What keeps you here?"

"I'm protected," she answered. "There's security within these walls."

He thought about that for a moment before continuing. "They come here because it's Cody Butler's shrine. If you moved away, to another house or even an apartment, they would stay here at the shrine; they wouldn't follow you.''

"It's not that simple, Nick," she said, but she was aware that some of what he said was true. She'd often thought of leaving, and yet something had kept her from breaking loose or, as Nick might put it, breaking free.

"No, I'm sure it's not." He was tempted to push her, only because he cared for her so much and wanted to help her make a change. Yet that was selfish of him, Nick knew, for he wanted it as much for himself as for her, and whatever decisions Ella made would have to be hers alone. If he pushed, he could lose her completely. He let the subject drop and gave himself to the day with her.

A wonderful day it was, with a real Mexican feast prepared by Juanita, who'd fallen completely under Nick's spell, and shared by Nikki, who was just as pleased as Juanita that Nick and Ella had found each other.

"I like him better each time I see him," Nikki declared when she and Ella left for a few minutes to tackle the last of the paperwork on Ella's desk. "He's so sophisticated." Nikki, who'd spent most of her life around show business, knew the difference between Hollywood sleek and inbred quality.

Ella handed Nikki the letters she'd signed. "There's a problem."

"With one of the letters?" Nikki asked.

Ella laughed. "No, with Nick's sophisticated background. Eventually I'm going to have to meet his family, Nikki."

"So?"

"My small-town childhood isn't so worrisome; it's what came after, the way I *looked*, Nikki. Don't you remember?"

"That was a long time ago."

"I'm afraid the world hasn't forgotten, and the senior Mannings still live in the world."

"I beg to differ with you, Ella. People like that don't pay any attention to what goes on out here in Lotusland."

"I hope you're right," Ella said. "I'm probably getting ahead of myself, anyway. He hasn't even asked me to meet his parents."

He asked her that night after Nikki left. Nick knew that she'd be hesitant, but the future was very much on his mind, probably because he saw so much uncertainty there. He needed some answers. "Neither of us knows what's going to happen. I'm not even sure of my plans with the State Department, but we can take it slowly, step by step. The first step, after my debriefing in Washington, is for me to go down to Fox Haven and for you to join me there."

Ella reluctantly agreed, but she was still unsure of herself, and Nick noted that immediately.

"There's nothing to worry about," he told her. "The old folks just take a little getting used to."

"That's not what I'm worried about; it's me. How long will it take your parents to get used to *me*?"

"About two seconds. Which is a second longer than it took me," he answered, giving her a hug. "You'll find out."

By the time the night ended, Ella was certain that she'd never have the chance to find out. Well before midnight, Nick had booked a flight to Washington on the red-eye and was in a cab headed for the airport.

When he looked back on what had happened, Nick realized that he had reacted abruptly, almost without thinking, which wasn't usual for the cool-headed diplomat. But the cool-headed diplomat had never been in such a bizarre situation, for he'd ended the night in a confrontation over a movie theater opening.

It seemed to him that Ella's actions proved she would always remain at La Casa, cemented to a pedestal, a statue moving only in moments of tribute to the ghost of her celebrity husband. He was capable of many things, but he couldn't fight that kind of competition.

It had begun the moment they arrived at La Casa and culminated with the appearance of Art Newcombe much later, while Ella and Nick were finishing their coffee and brandy in front of a fire. She seemed more relaxed, and Nick was certainly more comfortable. The day by the pool had brought back the memories of Balboa and with them the familiar ease they first found together. But Art's abrupt entrance had ended that.

He was a short, slight man in his fifties, with pale blond hair and light, almost eerie, blue eyes that saw everything and showed nothing. He paused long enough to be introduced to Nick, flashed a smile that revealed perfectly capped teeth, and extended a be-ringed hand. Then the hand was quickly withdrawn, and the smile disappeared as Art's cigarette was returned to its original place in the corner of his mouth, gripped between perfect teeth.

Nick felt an almost immediate, gut-level antipathy to Art Newcombe, and he knew instinctively that his feelings were reciprocated. He didn't care. It was obvious that the man was using Ella to line his own pockets.

"I'm sure that Mr. Manning will excuse us," Art suggested. "I need to talk to you, Ella. Something serious has come up." He led Ella toward the library door. "I have to take a lunch with the movie theater people tomorrow, and my girl tells me you've refused to attend the opening." His voice trailed off as they left the library and continued down the hall with Ella apologizing to Nick over her shoulder and assuring him they'd only be a few minutes.

It was a volatile few minutes of heated conversation that drifted clearly to Nick as he waited in the library. He remembered it in snatches.

Art began with a gentle berating of Ella for having Nick at La Casa. "It's too soon for another man to be coming here, darling," he told her almost sweetly.

"It's been two years, Art," she answered, "and Nick isn't another man; he's a very special friend."

"Even worse," came Art's reply.

The rest of the conversation concerned the theater opening. At first Ella was adamant in her refusal, which Art took as a personal affront, if not an outright sacrilege.

"Darling girl, this theater is named for Cody. One of the four screening rooms will be used exclusively for showing his movies. Once a week they'll run the documentary of his life. This is for Cody, Ella, not you or me. These people have gone all out for him. We can't back out now."

"I'm not making any personal appearances for a while," Ella explained calmly.

As he listened, Nick began to fear that she would relent. He wanted to step in and help her stay firm, but it was time for Ella to show her stuff. He waited for her to say no to Art.

But the pull of the past combined with Art's clever manipulation of guilt was too much for Ella. "Remember that Cody's birthday is coming up. We can't forget him, Ella, and we can't let down his fans. You're their lifeline to Cody," Art reminded her finally, and that seemed to clinch it. As he waited for Ella to give in, Nick couldn't help thinking of the dead men whose birthdays were still celebrated—men like Washington and Lincoln—and he had a hard time equating them with Cody Butler.

But the die had been cast. Ella had stepped back on her pedestal, and Nick wasn't about to climb up there with her. When she came back from her meeting with Art, Nick could read defeat on her face, triumph on Art's. The first battle had been fought and Art was clearly the victor.

It all hit Nick then, like a fist in his stomach: the shrinelike atmosphere of La Casa, Ella's uneasiness at his presence, the sudden interference of Art Newcombe.

Nick couldn't control the angry words that slipped out after Art left. "You really don't want to change, do you, Ella?"

"Yes, I do, Nick, but . . ."

He forced himself not to react to the pain in her eyes. "You've made your choice and given me an answer. I should have known the minute I stepped into this house." He knew he was overreacting, but this was one of the few times in his life when Nick couldn't control his emotions. "I sure as hell don't plan to live in another man's shadow, Ella, certainly not that of a dead rock star, no matter how famous. I'm not going to compete with him for your time." He turned and started up the stairs under the huge portrait of Cody Butler and his ever-watchful gaze. "And now I'd appreciate one of your *staff* calling me a taxi...."

During the next few days in Washington, Nick thought back in amazement at his behavior that night. He met with his superiors at State, going through the debriefing and trying to keep his mind on his work, but it was difficult, much more difficult than he'd imagined it would be. There was no doubt about it; Nick Manning had met the woman who would play a major role in his life, and all the celebrity-worshippers, all the hype, all the managers in California, wouldn't be able to keep him away from her—that is, if she would be willing to accept his apology for the way he'd left.

"There's nothing to talk about really, Nikki," Ella said when her friend questioned her two days after Nick's departure. "He's not interested in living in Cody's shadow, and I can't blame him." The fiasco of Nick's visit had been on her mind constantly, but she couldn't bear to rehash the scene with Nikki. It was too painfully intense.

Nikki had the good sense not to pry. Instead, she said matter-of-factly. "Then get out of the shadow yourself, Ella."

"I'm trying to, but it isn't easy, Nikki. Just look around you."

They were in Ella's office, where she'd finally caught up with all the mail and messages left over from her vacation, but more were piling up, because she hadn't been able to work since Nick left.

"See what happens in just two days?" She indicated the new accumulation.

"You can walk away from it, Ella."

"Believe me, I'm trying to, but it can't happen overnight." She gave a little sigh and then confessed something that had been bothering her for longer than she wanted to admit. "Maybe I'm afraid. Maybe I don't want to leave the comfort of this cocoon Cody spun around me."

"That's ridiculous," Nikki replied. "A few years ago I would have paid attention to that kind of talk, but not today. You were going through a growing process even while you were with Cody, but since his death you've begun to be your own person. Nick has just helped that along."

"I hope I have what it takes to continue on my own."

Nikki patted Ella's hand before she turned back to the typewriter. "You do," she answered, "but something tells me you aren't going to be on your own for long."

The phone rang, and Nikki picked it up, listening with a smile on her face. "Am I psychic or not?" she asked Ella as she handed her the receiver. "It's Nick."

Ella's heart was racing even before she heard his voice. She didn't notice Nikki leaving the room.

"I'm sorry for going off like that," he said. "I overreacted to say the least. You know why," he went on, not waiting for her response. "It's because I care so damned much. I'm so vulnerable where you're concerned, Ella."

"I understand," Ella told him, "and I care about you, too, Nick. I'm trying to get free of all this at La Casa, but it's much harder than I ever imagined."

"I know," he assured her, "and I won't rush you, but that doesn't mean I can stay away from you, Ella. It's been hell these past two days. I want to see you again and soon."

"I want to see you, Nick, but where? Not La Casa again." Ella didn't think she ever wanted to be in this house with Nick. It was Cody's house and always would be.

"We'll think of a place."

"Wherever it is, I'll still be recognized," she warned him.

"Don't worry about that," he told her. "I have a plan."

Chapter 6

Ella's excitement over the plan that Nick had initiated was momentarily forgotten when she saw the kids. It had been a long time for them and for Ella, too. Donnie's freckled face was the first thing she saw as she walked into the gym in the Cody Butler Wing of the hospital. In a matter of seconds he was in her arms, hanging on to her neck fiercely.

"Where've you been, Ella? Old Mrs. Robertson is no fun," he declared.

Ella gave him a big kiss and managed to pry herself from his grip to greet the other, less demonstrative kids.

"I've been on vacation," she told them, "and I understand that contrary to Donnie's report Mrs. Robertson did a great job while I was gone." Ignoring the moans, she continued, telling Donnie, "I understand you've improved so much you'll be playing basket-ball with your friends in another few weeks."

"Maybe so," the boy admitted, "but she's no *fun*."

"We don't play games. We just do exercises the whole hour," another child piped up.

"Today we'll do both," Ella promised.

She was true to her word, taking the kids through their regime, which she interspersed with the games they enjoyed so much, and staying on with them an extra half hour until both she and the kids were exhausted. Finally, Ella managed to bring the class to a close with a promise that she wouldn't stay away so long the next time.

"Or if you do, get somebody else to take your place."

"Yeah, we don't like old lady Robertson."

"She's no *fun*," Donnie repeated.

Ella was still laughing as she walked down the hall to Susan's office. Old lady Robertson was all of twenty-five.

"Maybe you should give Sandy Robertson a list of the games you play with the kids," Susan suggested as Ella collapsed in an office chair.

"I don't have any idea what they are, Susan. I just make up little routines as we go along and cram the required exercises in between."

Susan laughed. "That's why you're so good, Ella. It's talent, not training. Maybe I'll peep in tomorrow and see what Sandy's missing."

"They've all improved since I've been gone," Ella assured her, "so Sandy's doing quite well. She just needs to have a little more *fun* with them, as Donnie says."

"Which can't be taught," a voice declared from the doorway. Dr. Douglas Dunne entered, went over to Ella and gave her a kiss. "You look great. Susan tells me you had a wonderful vacation."

"I did," Ella said. "Balboa is beautiful, an almost perfect place."

"Almost?" Doug settled into the chair next to Ella. He was a burly man with a disheveled appearance, rumpled clothes and equally rumpled hair. Susan always claimed that her husband looked like a medical student after a twenty-four-hour shift. His hands and face were scrubbed clean, and his clothes were spotless; they just looked slept-in. "What makes it *almost* paradise?" he asked Ella.

"There's something missing," Ella told him. "It wouldn't be a good place to get sick."

"No hospital?" Susan asked.

Ella almost laughed. "Not only is there no hospital; there's barely a clinic. It's on Kikao, and the doctor from Balboa visits it periodically. The rest of the time he's at Paradise Cove, treating minor ailments among the resort guests. If the islanders want to see him, they have to go to Kikao and wait. I never did determine how long the wait might be."

"Oh, that *is* too bad," Susan said, "for the island families, especially the children."

"I want to do something about it," Ella said determinedly.

Doug and Susan looked at each other and waited.

"It wouldn't cost an exorbitant amount to build a small hospital there and staff it adequately. Just a doctor and a couple of nurses would be sufficient as long they were there all the time."

"And you're thinking of taking the project on?" Doug guessed.

"It's not such a farfetched idea," Ella said defensively. "The money is certainly available in Cody's trust. All that's needed to get started is expert advice, preferably from one of the doctors who attended the conference on child care clinics."

"Who did you have in mind, exactly?" Doug asked, a grin on his wide face.

"Well..."

"Oh, no," Susan began.

"Wait. Let's hear her out," Doug suggested.

"All you have to do is hire someone to fly down and look over the situation, get the facts and figures and present them to you in a feasibility study."

Susan was skeptical. "After only one visit, Ella, this seems somewhat premature. Are you sure about a doctor? Maybe on some of the other islands—"

"I'm sure," Ella said. "When I got back from Kikao I talked to a number of people, both at the resort and in town. Then I met the doctor. He's not exactly Dr. Schweitzer. He knows how to treat a bad cold, and that's about it, as far as I can tell. I wouldn't want to say he's an alcoholic, but he's most often seen at Parae Cove during cocktail hour. Hardly the person I'd want to entrust my family to if I lived on those islands," Ella said adamantly.

Susan looked over at Doug for his reaction, which was getting more and more favorable. "It certainly could be a choice spot to put some of our findings to work," he said with a smile to Ella. "You should be an administrator, with all you've learned over the past couple of years at the hospital."

"Not to mention her persuasiveness," Susan added.

"Yes, she's certainly made it sound enticing. We could hire a firm to do the study. There were several groups at the conference who specialize in this sort of preliminary work. Armed with the input from the child care clinics we studied last week, there shouldn't be any problem getting what we need for feasibility."

A smile was tugging at Susan's lips.

"What's so funny?" her husband asked.

"Not funny; tempting," she answered. "You and I are due for a vacation, Doug..."

"A little overdue," Doug put in.

"And you certainly have all the expertise that's needed for this kind of assignment," Ella added.

"We could combine business and pleasure," Susan said, her smile turning into a broad grin.

"It's a perfect solution," Ella exclaimed. "There's no one whose opinion I respect more."

"It certainly sounds tempting," Doug said. "Are you seriously considering this?" he asked his wife.

Ella was aware that Susan was usually more cautious than her husband. If *she* thought the trip was a good idea, chances were they'd go. Ella waited for the response.

"I'm enchanted by it. Besides, I could use a taste of island paradise," she added, but Ella also caught the serious look on her friend's face. Dr. Susan Dunne was ready to go to work.

"Then we'll go," Doug agreed.

"I'll pick up the tab," Ella volunteered.

Doug shook his head. "Nope. You do enough for us. This one's on the Dunnes. We'll leave at the end of the week."

"Great," Ella said. "I think you'll agree with my assessment. I can almost see the hospital now. For me, it's already a reality."

Doug laughed. "As I said, you'd be a great administrator."

"I learned it all from you two, and now I have one more favor to ask."

"Name it," Susan responded.

"Trade places with me."

"Who?" Doug asked.

"Not you. Your wife," Ella said with a grin. "I'd like us to exchange identities, Susan. Oh, don't worry, not forever. Just for this afternoon."

"I'm waiting for an explanation of this request," Doug said, settling back in his chair and lighting his pipe.

Ella felt a blush rising to her cheeks. "I want to meet someone, a…friend, and I want to avoid publicity, if possible. So I thought if I left the hospital driving Susan's car and she went home in mine, the press might be fooled for a while."

"Have they been watching you?" Susan asked.

"Yes, more carefully than ever. They're on to the fact that I'm seeing someone. He was here for a couple of days," she explained, "and I suspect one of the little spies at the La Casa gates blew the whistle."

"Let's backtrack a moment," Susan suggested. "I assume this friend is a man?"

Ella nodded.

"And he visited you at La Casa?"

She nodded again.

A glimmer lit Susan's eyes. "I had a feeling something special happened on Balboa besides the nice weather. He's the reason you stayed over?" she guessed.

Ella nodded. "When we left Balboa he came back to La Casa, which wasn't paradise, to say the least."

"I guess not," Susan agreed. "La Casa isn't exactly off the beaten path for Cody worshipers."

"We've decided to get away to somewhere less obvious. He's planned it all very carefully."

"Let's hear about him," Doug suggested. Ella saw the look in his eye and realized again how much the Dunnes cared about her. They'd always thought she deserved more than a life as Cody's widow.

"His name is Nicholas Manning," Ella explained. "He's a diplomat just returning from an assignment overseas. As you might guess, he's different from anyone I've ever known, and I like him very much."

"Oh, that's wonderful," Susan said, "and I'm for anything that will get you away from La Casa and give you some privacy for a change. Tell me what I can do."

Ella dug into her large tote bag and pulled out a gray wig. "Nikki picked this up for me. With the wig in place, these glasses," she said, extracting steel-framed glasses from the tote, "and a white hospital coat, I can pass for Susan, especially behind the wheel of her car. Anyone watching the hospital will just think Dr. Dunne is going home."

"A great idea," Susan said, laughing as Ella plopped the wig on her head.

"Then can I borrow your car?"

"For as long as you'd like. Meanwhile, Cal can take me home in the limo."

Ella had a better idea. "No, someone might notice. I probably sound paranoid, but I don't want anything to spoil this weekend with Nick. So here's the plan...." She leaned forward conspiratorially, and both Doug and Susan followed suit, all three smiling with delight. "Cal will wait until you get off work and drive you to La Casa." She fished into her tote again. "If you wear dark glasses and a scarf you won't even be noticed in the back seat of the limo. I've asked Juanita to prepare dinner for two. Doug can join you and drive you home after dinner or you can spend the night. As you know, there's a plentiful choice of bedrooms." Ella sat back in the chair and looked at them expectantly. "Do you think it'll work?"

They responded affirmatively and laughed again at Ella, so childishly full of fun. She had managed to get the wig in place and put on the prop glasses. Doug helped her into Susan's white coat, and she was ready.

Susan handed her the keys and gave her a hug. "I guess we'd better start the ruse here in case there are spies in the halls."

"Okay," Ella said, throwing back her shoulders and assuming what they all decided was a medical air—serious and worried. "From this moment, I'm Dr. Susan Dunne. Wish me luck."

As soon as she stepped into the hall, Ella began to feel self-conscious, but the feeling didn't last long, because no one gave her a second look. She made her way to the parking garage and Susan's car, wig and glasses in place, her medical demeanor equally secure.

Starting the engine, Ella experienced a little thrill. She was used to being chauffeured and couldn't even remember the last time she'd been behind a wheel. "I hope I remember how to do this," she said aloud as she turned the key and eased out of the parking place.

When she reached the street, Ella stopped and pulled over to acquaint herself with the car, something she realized should have preceded the turning of the key. Finally, sure that she knew where everything was located, she merged into the traffic and headed for the freeway.

It was a long drive to the hideaway Nick had located for them, and before she was halfway there, Ella was feeling quite comfortable and able to give herself over to thoughts of what lay ahead. Anticipation was mixed with nervousness. They would be secluded, away from press and fans, but in a real setting, not in the fantasy of Paradise Cove, not behind the walls of La Casa but in an ordinary house in an ordinary town.

The house belonged to a friend of Nick's who was in the Middle East for six months. The house was in a small town in the foothills west of Los Angeles. Even though she'd spent twelve years in California, Ella had no idea what to expect. She rarely ventured far from the city and had never even been on the freeway that took her to Yorba Linda. Looking around as she drove, she was not terribly impressed. The countryside, what she could see of it, was arid and uninteresting, but as she turned off to the town, her surroundings improved.

The houses were far apart, not crammed on top of one another as in much of California, and there were orchards everywhere—orange, grapefruit, lemon and avocado trees springing up from the arid ground and watered by irrigation systems. The fruit hung abun-

dantly from the trees along the road, and as she got
closer to her destination, Ella passed as many people
on horseback as in cars.

Following the directions Nick had given her, Ella
managed to get lost immediately, and after driving for
twenty minutes she finally gave in and stopped at a
minigrocery to ask directions. When she got out of the
car, Ella automatically shied away from the knot of
people gathered at the soft drink machine. She was
afraid of being recognized, but no one even glanced
her way. The disguise worked, she thought as she
boldly marched into the store, where the owner interpreted her makeshift map and pointed her in the right
direction. She thanked him, bought a drink and lingered for a few minutes, listening to the talk of the
weather, the crops and the possibility of earthquakes,
feeling like a normal human being for a change.

After she finished her drink and headed for the car,
they all said goodbye, good luck in finding her way,
and one of the men called her ''doc.'' Until then Ella
hadn't been aware of the name tag on her hospital coat
that identified her as Dr. Dunne.

There was a nip in the air at Yorba Linda, and Nick
had lit the logs in the stone fireplace, fixed himself a
drink and settled down to wait for Ella. It was a long
wait, and as the hour when he'd expected her came
and went, Nick began to get nervous. He couldn't help
thinking of how he'd left her at La Casa, his arro-
gance and lack of understanding. Even though she'd
seemed excited about this meeting, as the minutes
passed he began to wonder if she was coming. The
doubt soon gave way to worry. Something could have

happened to her. Ella wasn't used to driving, especially on unfamiliar freeways.

He put down his drink, went to the phone, and called La Casa. Nikki answered, assured him that Ella had left the hospital and was on the way.

"She probably got lost," Nikki told him. "Ella was never great with directions, even on familiar terrain. Don't fret, Nick; she'll be there."

Somewhat appeased, he sat back down in front of the fire and let his imagination take over. He envisioned her walking into the room, her brown hair shining in the firelight. He could see her reach up and brush a lock away from her face, tucking it behind her ear as he'd watched her do a dozen times. Her blue eyes sparkled; her red lips parted and spoke his name. He could almost feel the taste of her mouth against his.

Completely lost in this vision, at first Nick didn't hear the car pull up into the driveway. Then there was an almost timid beep of the horn. He got up like a shot and rushed to the front door.

Coming toward him wasn't exactly the vision of his overactive imagination but a woman in a loose-fitting white hospital coat, her shining brown hair covered by a gray wig, her blue eyes behind steel-rimmed glasses. Nick started to laugh.

Ella realized how she looked to him and pulled off the wig to let her hair tumble to her shoulders. He took the glasses off for her as she stepped into his arms, and the kiss that followed was much more than the one he'd just lived through vicariously. When it ended, he looked down at her and saw on her face an expression of vulnerability and hope and nervousness. His heart lurched in his chest. She was so honest with her emotions.

"Oh, Ella, Ella," he whispered, kissing her again and again. He didn't want to stop, but something told him it was best not to rush her. Just having her with him again was a victory of sorts. "I'm so glad you're here," he whispered.

"I'm glad, too." She took his arm and walked beside him into the house. "Everything worked perfectly. No one suspected. I got lost—"

"Nikki said you would."

"Did you call Nikki?"

"I was getting worried about you," he explained.

"Well, I had a marvelous time. Chatted with all the folks at the grocery store. One of them called me 'doc.' Oh, it was great!"

Ella was obviously full of herself, and Nick laughed at the sheer joy of having her with him. "You're like no one else in the world, no other woman I've ever met." He kissed her once more and took her bag. "Let me show you our hideaway."

He took her on a tour of the rambling house, through the huge living room, down the hall to the library and the guest bedroom and upstairs to the master bedroom. It was rustic and very homey, with paneled walls, a Navajo white ceiling and exposed beams. The view through the floor-to-ceiling windows was the verdant orchards. There wasn't another house in sight.

He put her bag down and said simply, "This will be our room."

The pause was long and for Nick filled with a few seconds of doubt. He knew she was happy to see him, but he thought he saw hesitation in her eyes. He would need to go slowly in order to bring them what they'd had before La Casa, to gain her confidence. Nick wasn't sure he understood her completely, but she was a complicated woman and theirs was proving to be a complicated love affair. He was determined that they would survive whatever obstacles were put in their way, and he made a silent promise not to put any there himself.

"Come on," he said, taking her hand. "Let's go down and sit by the fire while it's still burning. I lit it a long time ago, not expecting you to get lost."

Two hours later they were still sitting in front of the fire, sipping wine and talking. He'd told her about the goings-on at the Capitol, the uninteresting dinner party he'd attended for a senator friend, where he'd thought of nothing all evening except her. "I even thought about you during the debriefing. I expect it was somewhat disconcerting for my superiors," he told her with a laugh. But he avoided any mention of the scene at La Casa. He had apologized; she had accepted his apology, and he hoped La Casa and Art Newcombe were well behind them. He was still convinced that her fears of public harassment were unfounded, but even if there was a sound basis for her worries, every day that passed was in their favor. Time was on their side. Meanwhile, they'd be together as much as possible. Nick intended to see to that.

"We don't need Balboa," he said to her after a long, comfortable silence during which they'd sat side by side, their backs against the sofa, looking into the dying fire. "Anywhere you are looks like Paradise Cove to me. Even Yorba Linda, California."

"I like it here," she assured him. "It's a nice town, and I have a feeling I wouldn't even have to wear my disguise. If I were recognized, I don't think anyone would bother me."

"I'm sure you're right. We'll try out your theory tomorrow. But tomorrow's a long way off," he said, then covered her mouth with his kiss.

Her lips parted under his, and she felt herself melt, flow into him hotly, knowing that her whole body had been waiting for this moment. He moved his hand along the contours of her back, pulling her closer and closer until there was no space between them, just their two hungry, yearning bodies pressed together. Ella felt a sigh escape her lips. Only a week had passed, but even that had been too long. He planned for them to be together as much as possible during the next two months of his leave; he told her that, and Ella suddenly hoped with all her heart that he was right. Feeling as she did now, she couldn't imagine being without him.

Moving his hand under her sweater, Nick fumbled with the clasp of her bra. "Damn these clothes," he said as he finally managed to pull off her bra and the shirt she'd worn under Susan's hospital coat. "It was easier on Balboa without all the layers. No clothes, no..." His words stopped, because his mouth had found her taut pink nipple and closed around it.

Ella felt the sensation his mouth and tongue and teeth caused. It swept through her, turning her blood into liquid fire, and she knew they would never make it to the bedroom. She even wondered, during the split second her brain worked, if they would make it onto the sofa, but that thought had barely formed before it no longer mattered to her. While Ella shed the rest of her clothes with Nick's help, she was powerless to help him and could only watch as he undressed.

Once out of his clothes, he lifted her naked body against his and then onto the sofa, where she lay stretched out before him. Ella watched Nick as his eyes roamed her body, and she could almost feel the heat of his gaze. He seemed to be worshiping her with his eyes, and the pleasure that gave made her tremble with delight.

Almost reverently, Nick knelt down beside her, and his hands and lips followed the path his eyes had taken before, from the tips of her toes, across her instep to her calf, tasting and touching with delight. When his lips touched the inside of her thigh and continued a damp path to the feathery curls that covered her femininity, she caught her breath and gasped aloud. But he didn't stop there; his exploration continued upward along her ribs over the line of her tan, across the white bikini band to her breasts.

By the time his mouth captured her nipple again, Ella's emotions were spinning, her only reality the sensation of Nick's lips on her skin. Her flesh was hot and feverish, every nerve ending alive and on fire.

She reached out and wrapped her fingers in his thick, crisp hair, holding him to her breast. His tongue was magic, teasing, taunting, tantalizing, until she thought her body would explode. Unable to control the spasms of pleasure that slithered through her, she gave herself to them and to the whimpers they caused deep in her throat, holding nothing back.

Nick reacted to her fervor with a kiss more probing than before. His tongue filled her mouth, met hers, touched, meshed and melded as their bodies molded flesh to flesh and then, in a moment that jarred them both with its intensity, he entered her. That moment wrapped them in passion that threatened never to end, defying nature with its forcefulness and magnitude, for he plunged to her depths and then seemed to go even deeper. She lifted her hips to meet him and accept the shaft of his love and desire, holding him inside with spasms that went on and on until the end came at last.

It carried them higher than ever before, shaking their bodies with such violence that the very air seemed to quake with the force of their final shattering convulsion. When it was over, Ella held on to him until the room stopped spinning and she could feel the fabric of the sofa beneath her. When that happened she knew that they were still there even though it had seemed that they had been flung away to some other sphere.

Then once more it happened for her as he placed his hands beneath her hips and brought her up against him, causing another spasm. She cried out then in surprise and ecstasy, and his mouth covered her cry, halting it but not halting the delirium that overcame her. Digging her nails into his back, she felt her body go out of control again.

"Yes, yes, Ella," he answered, covering her mouth with his once more and leaving it covered until at last, this time finally, she was still.

Time had no meaning for Ella. She only knew that when he spoke again her body was cool although still damp, and her heart had stopped racing. She was calm, peaceful.

"You're beautiful," he told her, pushing back a wave of damp hair from her forehead. "And wonderful."

"And very happy," she added.

"Is this enough to make you happy?"

"Being with you? yes," she answered. "We're together and we...care about each other." She couldn't say *love* yet.

His heart had stopped for a moment as he waited for her to say the word that would make it all complete. It didn't come, so he held it back himself. He'd already told her how he felt; now he would just have to wait for her response. Physically and in every other way, they were perfectly suited; he wanted no one but Ella, now or ever. She was more cautious. He wouldn't push.

After a big stretch, he got up, pulled on his rumpled cords and gave her bare bottom an affectionate pat. "Did you bring a robe?"

She nodded. "It's in my bag."

"I'll bring it down to you. Then we need to wind our way into the kitchen. It's well past suppertime, and I'm starved." With that, he left her by what remained of the fire and went upstairs, returning with her robe.

"It's much sexier than the hospital coat," he said, wrapping her in the blue terry cloth. "No, don't pull it around your throat like that." He opened the collar until her breasts were partially exposed, and then smiled. "There. That's better. Now, into the kitchen."

"I bet you think I can't cook," she said, looking up at him impudently.

"Actually, I hadn't even wondered about your culinary talents. Everything else about you is so perfect, it's possible that you can even cook. However," he added, leading her into the kitchen, "I doubt that you had much practice at La Casa, with Juanita and all of her staff wielding their pots and pans."

"True," Ella admitted, "but I *can* cook. Remember, I was Ella Kincaid from Tyler, Texas. I make a mean chili, the crispiest fried chicken west of the Mississippi, and of course, deep-dish apple pie."

"The girl of my dreams," Nick said, handing her a skillet. "But tonight it's enchiladas. You brown the meat and I'll sauté the tortillas."

"I hope you have olives and salsa," Ella said as she went about her task.

"Naturally," Nick declared. "Olives ripe off the tree and salsa from the grocery store shelf. A good combination."

Ella watched Nick dip the tortillas in hot oil and spread them on paper towels.

"I believe I detect some real expertise there," she said admiringly.

"I've always had a cook on my posts abroad, but often I've had to teach them to prepare meals that I could eat. The local fare didn't always suit my palate. I'm especially fond of Mexican, for instance. As Juanita will confirm."

"Oh, yes. You have a big fan there."

"I hope so," Nick said. "Maybe she'll sway you in my direction. As for me, I don't need swaying," he continued, planting a kiss on her cheek between tortillas. "I only cook for those I love." Nick said that as a throwaway line, and she took it as such even though his meaning was much deeper.

"Well, I haven't cooked for *anyone* in ages. I used to go into the kitchen occasionally, and Juanita would let me make meals for myself."

"Not for Cody?" he asked.

"Cody didn't want me to cook, probably because he grew up so poor, in foster homes and orphanages. When he became successful, he wanted to live the kind of existence he'd seen in the movies that had sustained him when he was a child. Sometimes I'd bake a pie for him or a cake for his birthday, but he never went near the kitchen." She laughed in remembrance. "Often when he wanted something special he sent the plane for it—ribs from Chicago or Cajun from New Orleans. He thought it was easier to fly a meal in than go near the kitchen on Juanita's day off."

"Yet you managed to stay so unspoiled," Nick said in wonder.

"I'm far from perfect, Nick. You need to understand that. I'm no saint."

"Which suits me fine," he said, "because neither am I." He quirked an eyebrow. "As you may remember from our adventure on the sofa."

They were silent for a few moments while they finished preparing the enchiladas and took their plates to the table. "We're a good team," he said, repeating the observation he'd first made on Balboa. "You're an easy person to be with. Cody Butler was a lucky man."

"That marriage wasn't perfect, either," she said after a thoughtful moment.

"Few are," he answered.

"Especially when success is so much a part of the life-style. Money and fame can be accompanied by serious problems. During the last couple of years, it was very difficult. Cody had begun to drink," she said, admitting what she'd kept from him before. "Few people knew about that. Nikki, Art, our lawyer, Cody's doctor. I tried to help, but that just made everything worse. He wasn't ready to admit that he was an alcoholic. He became belligerent. The last year was terrible," she said.

"I'm sorry, Ella. I didn't know." He reached for her hand across the table. "Is that why you're shy of marriage now?"

"It's one of the reasons, Nick. You know the other one. I went from a child to a woman as Cody's wife, no more than an appendage of a famous star. I'm trying to make the break that will put me on my own."

"I know you are, and I want to help."

"I may need to do this alone," she told him.

"Does that also mean you're not ready for another serious relationship?" He had to ask that, bring it into the open. "Even if I stand aside and let you grow?"

"I'm not sure, Nick."

He didn't like what he was hearing. "I think you are, Ella. I think now is the time, and I'm the man." The look on his face was as intent as the tone of his voice. "Tell me that you don't care for me."

"You know I care," she answered.

"Then tell me you're going to give us a chance."

"I'm here, aren't I?"

"Yes, you're here," he said with a smile, "and for now that will have to be enough. But I want a wife and family. I knew when I came home I needed that, and

I knew when I met you I'd found my future. I'm a pretty determined man, Ella.''

Ella smiled at him across the table and tried not to think that Cody, too, had been determined.

Chapter 7

She'd never spent a day quite like it. During her childhood, Ella's days had passed in such an ordinary way that she'd had trouble later even remembering them. As Cody's wife, she'd lived what they'd referred to as "an adventure in hiding." It was usually exciting, always active, often entertaining and certainly never dull. Her day with Nick in Yorba Linda had been so *normal*. That was the word Nick kept using, but for Ella, who'd rarely experienced normalcy, it was unique.

They woke up surrounded by the sight and scent of the orchards, dressed and walked outside to pick grapefruit for their breakfast, followed by two Labrador retrievers. The dogs, along with assorted cats, a pair of doves that lived in the greenhouse and a dozen or so chickens, made up the animal population of the place.

"Who takes care of this menagerie when your friend's traveling?" Ella asked.

"A woman who lives up the road comes by and feeds them every day and collects the eggs from the setting hens."

"And picks the fruit, I suppose," Ella said, choosing a plump grapefruit that had just fallen from the tree. "This'll be my breakfast."

"Actually, the neighbors keep the orchard picked. There's a jar over in the shed by the main road where they leave money for the fruit. Or they trade with chores. One old fellow moves the hoses around and keeps the irrigation system running. Otherwise, the farm takes care of itself."

Ella shook her head in wonder. It all seemed so easy. She thought of her gardeners bustling around, working all day to keep the flowers and the yard looking just right, while all these acres seemed to tend themselves with a little help from neighbors.

After breakfast they took a long walk with the dogs, stopping to rest in the shade of an avocado tree. "I've never seen anything like this," Ella exclaimed as they ducked under the branches and found themselves standing upright in an area as large as a room with low limbs swooping down to form a canopy around them.

"It's like a miniature castle under here," Ella exclaimed. "I feel like I could stay forever." She plopped down and leaned against the huge tree trunk.

Nick settled beside her. "Not forever, I hope. I have other permanent plans for you."

Ella didn't respond to that. She hadn't responded to any of his references about their future, because she was still so uncertain about *herself*. Until she found the direction of her own life, she couldn't think of sharing it with anyone else. Nick had made all of his remarks lightly and didn't seem to notice her lack of response. He certainly made conversation easy for her, Ella thought. Suddenly she decided to tell him about her plans for the hospital in the islands.

He listened and didn't seem at all surprised. "I had a feeling something was cooking in your mind when you stopped to hang around that clinic."

"Clinic is a very flattering term," she said. "The equipment in there was no better than you'd find at a Boy Scout camp-out. I'm going to build a facility and supply it properly."

"If, as you were told, there's only one doctor in the area—"

"And he's an alcoholic," Ella added.

"Then who's going to staff the hospital?" he finished.

"I don't think we'll have any problem getting a medical team. The island setting should attract an endless string of qualified doctors and nurses."

Nick had to agree with that assessment.

"I've been thinking of converting that old villa," she continued, "and putting the clinic on Kikao. It's not as big as Balboa, but it has a larger population and is more accessible to the other islands. With the motor launches available, all we'd need is a couple of jeeps to get up to the villa. That would make it easy for guests at Paradise Cove. Wherever there are good medical facilities, rich people tend to get sick more easily. The fees we could charge them would help pay good salaries for the staff."

"What a little schemer you are," he said, putting his arms around Ella and giving her a kiss on the top of the head. "But it's a good scheme and maybe your way to break loose from being Cody's widow."

"I hope so," she said seriously.

"Pretty soon you'll be just plain old Ella Butler, and people will stop making the connection."

"Fans can be pretty persistent, not to mention the press."

"All the dedicated groupies are in Los Angeles, Ella. An occasional fan is no problem. Neither is an occasional reporter."

Ella laughed. "I'm afraid I've never run into the 'occasional' reporter. They seem to come in packs."

"Not where 'normal' folks live. Come on," he said, standing up and taking her hand. "We'll go into Yorba Linda and I'll prove it. You can be a normal person, live a normal life. It's probably a good time to leave this castle anyway, since the ants are crawling all over."

"I know," Ella said as she let him pull her up and then bent down to brush at her bare legs. "I tried to ignore them and continue my fantasy about the castle."

"We've ended fantasies, remember?" He pulled her out from under the tree and into the bright sunlight. "This is reality. It's where you're going to work everything out. I just don't like the idea that we live so far apart, that you have to be a continent away from me while you're working it out."

"This is the jet age," she reminded him.

"Yes, I know, and you have a jet—which does make things easier. However," he said, brushing away what he hoped was a final ant, "for transportation to town today, I suggest feet."

"Agreed," Ella said, striding briskly along beside him. "Do you think I need a disguise?"

Nick laughed. "I think what you have on is disguise enough." She was wearing a pair of old shorts, a shirt of Nick's that she'd tied at the waist and a baseball cap she'd picked up off a hat rack in the den. "We'll see if you attract attention, but if you do, I think it'll be because of the peculiarity of the outfit."

"Peculiar?" she said with mock astonishment. "I think I look downright cute. Which I suppose is a little silly at my age."

He gave the baseball cap a yank. "You'll be cute when you're a hundred."

Nick was right about Ella not being recognized. They were the recipients of a few waves as they walked to town, waves not of recognition but of acknowledgment. They were simply strangers in a friendly place. They shopped at the supermarket, browsed at a book store and stopped on the way home for ice-cream cones. The dogs went with them everywhere and were the only ones recognized.

"Upstaged by a couple of Labs," Nick said with a laugh as they started the walk back.

"It's certainly a first," Ella admitted.

"And I hope an indicator of things to come."

The rest of their "normal" day consisted of lunch on the patio followed by a long nap and then a strenuous game of horseshoes in the backyard and visits by several neighbors who came to pick fruit and ended up joining the game. It was almost dark by the time everyone left, and Ella was exhilarated.

"I don't know when I've had so much fun," she said.

"I've always maintained that all it takes is a few good games of horseshoes to make life really interesting," Nick said.

"I'm not joking, Nick. I could get used to this normal kind of life."

"Stick with me, baby," he told her.

"But this isn't the kind of life you lead, or even want to lead," she reminded him.

"No, it isn't," he admitted. "This is only a respite. I like to be where I can make a difference or at least make a contribution toward easing some of the problems in the world. So do you, Ella," he reminded her. "In that way, we're very much alike. Do you want to grill steaks on the barbecue?" he asked, changing the subject.

"Yes," she said. "Light the charcoal and I'll get the steaks. Do you know what you're going to do next, Nick?"

"Light the charcoal, as per your orders."

"That's not what I mean. I'm talking about your career."

"I haven't made any decisions yet, Ella. I still have lots of time."

"I've made a decision," she told him.

He waited, hoping that he was a part of her plans.

"I'm going to start living again. I've already started," she amended, "and I like the way it feels. Thanks for giving me the push, Nick."

"Just remember, I'll be there if anything happens to drive you back into the cocoon. Now go get those steaks."

They went to bed early, right after dinner, and the dogs went with them, one of them sleeping at the foot of the bed, the other on the floor next to Ella. Nick got up twice during the night to put them outside so he and Ella could make love.

"Don't get me wrong," he told her, taking her in his arms. "I like animals, but there comes a time when..." The rest was lost in their kiss.

That first day set the tone for the rest of their long weekend, lazy and peaceful. Except for breakfast, their meals hadn't been outstanding, with over-cooked grilled steaks the low point. Nick decided they should eat lunch and dinner out, and Ella found a restaurant guide from which she selected the ones that sounded particularly appealing. By the third day they were driving long distances to satisfy her whims.

"You've been right on target so far," Nick said lazily while she flipped through the guide. "What's it going to be tonight?"

"How about a rustic rambling spot in the San Bernadino Mountains where the food is as down-home and satisfying as the setting?"

"Is that a direct quote?"

"Yep."

"I would guess that means I don't need to wear a tie," Nick said with a modicum of understatement.

"Jeans might even fit the bill."

"Then I'm ready to go."

"Nick, it's only five o'clock," she reminded him.

"It's a long drive, and I want to get back early."

"Why? Is there something urgent on your agenda?"

"Of course," he said with total seriousness. "A long walk through the orchards, a nightcap by the fire. And don't forget, we have to feed the animals before bed."

"It's a tough life," she said with a laugh.

Half an hour later, with Ella directing, they were lost. "This is ridiculous," Nick said, backing up at the end of a dirt road and turning around. "I've found my way out of jungles in the depths of Africa, but when Ella Butler gives directions I manage to get lost."

"Only in America," Ella said, holding back a giggle and carefully analyzing her map. "I think the mistake was at the next-to-last turn. We should have gone left."

"Which means you had the map upside down," he chided her lightly.

"You may be right," she admitted, "but I think I've got it all figured out now."

After only one more wrong turn, they arrived at the restaurant, which was all the guidebook had led them to believe. Not until the end of the delicious meal did Ella's mood change. She'd successfully fought back the feeling of foreboding that had threatened her from the beginning, but she couldn't fight it any longer. She knew quite suddenly and without a doubt that their idyll was almost over.

"What is it, Ella?" Nick asked, picking up her nervousness.

"It's nothing," she tried, and then knew it was useless to lie to him. "The maître d' has been watching me all night," she admitted.

"He probably thinks you're pretty," Nick said with a total lack of concern. "I know I do. Without the baseball cap you could even pass for beautiful."

Ella couldn't bring herself to laugh. She had a premonition, and she knew it wasn't groundless. She took a sip of coffee. "He's looking at me now."

"Maybe it's love at first sight." Nick finished his coffee and signaled for the bill.

"Be serious, Nick."

"I am serious. Remember the boat?"

She looked at him with a frown. "What boat?"

"Oh, how quickly they forget," he said with a grin. "The boat to Kikao. I fell in love with you at first sight."

Ella felt herself blushing and, as he reached across the table, forgetting all about the maître d'.

"That was a special moment for me," he told her.

"It was special for me, too," Ella said, remembering their first meeting.

"You probably thought I was a fan," Nick suggested. They'd discussed the meeting before, but never her reaction.

"I'm not sure what I was thinking," she said, "but I must admit my heart sped up considerably. Then when we were getting off the boat and you passed right by me, I decided that you recognized me and lost interest.

"Well, you certainly read that wrong, Ella, so there's a pretty good chance you're misreading the look on the maître d's face, too."

"No," she disagreed. "He recognizes me."

"There's nothing the matter with that," Nick told her.

"As long as he keeps it to himself," Ella said. But the warning signs were there, and they bothered her all the way home in spite of Nick's efforts to distract her.

Gradually Ella let her attention be diverted toward the evening chores. By the time the last of the animals was fed, she had forgotten all about the man in the restaurant, and by nine o'clock they were ready to put out the fire and go up to bed.

That's when the first of the vans appeared. Ella heard the noise of the engine, followed by the dogs barking. She went to the back window and looked out. Her startled gasp drew Nick to her side.

As the van emerged into the light from the house, he could see the TV station logo. "Damn," he cursed under his breath.

"The maître d' called them," Ella said flatly.

"Why?" Nick asked, showing his naivety.

"Oh, Nick," Ella said in an almost scolding voice. "I was on a date with a handsome, attentive man. That's news."

"No, Ella," Nick said gruffly. "War in the Persian Gulf is news. This is gossip, and I'm going to put an end to it."

"Nick," Ella said, catching hold of his sleeve, "maybe I should call Art."

He pulled away. "No. I've handled the press all over the world. I can certainly handle a van from a local TV station."

"Two vans," Ella corrected him as a second one pulled into the driveway. "And it's not a Yorba Linda station; it's Los Angeles."

"I'll get rid of them. The fact that you and I are spending a weekend together can't be worth all this."

Ella stepped aside without answering, but she couldn't help thinking that this was the beginning of the end for them.

Nick went outside and closed the door behind him. The dogs continued their barking, and Nick did nothing to stop them. Hesitantly, a middle-aged man climbed out of one of the vans, and a woman from the other. Nick called the dogs back and held them by their collars, not downplaying their apparent ferociousness. He decided to let the reporters think they were attack dogs; it couldn't hurt.

"Kathy Laborde, from KRAO," the woman said, not venturing far from the truck. "How long have you and Ella Butler been seeing each other?" She held the mike in his direction, tentatively.

Nick ignored the question. "You're trespassing on private property," he said calmly, "which makes me perfectly within my rights to release these dogs on you."

The woman stepped back a couple of feet; the man wasn't quite as timid. Holding his mike toward Nick, he began, "Mr. Manning—"

"How the hell do you know my name?" Nick asked.

"John McCormick, KWWL," the man said. "I was with the wire service a couple of years ago on the Afghan border. I recognized you." With that explanation he went on to what mattered. "This is a big story, Mr. Manning, you and Cody Butler's widow."

"This isn't a story at all, Mr. McCormick," Nick answered. "Nor have you any proof that Mrs. Butler is here."

"Ah, come on, Manning," the man said, inching closer in spite of the growling dogs. "We got positive ID from the guy who gave us the lead, and one of my boys picked up your car on the freeway and followed you here. Ella Butler's inside; there's no question about that," he added confidently.

"Where did you and Ella meet?" the woman asked.

"Ms. Laborde," Nick said, again avoiding the question, "I'm here on a private visit, and as I said before, this is private property. I'm going to ask you again, as politely as I can, to please leave."

Watching from inside, Ella could tell that Nick believed he could handle the situation; he didn't know what he was up against. Ella recognized both reporters. They thrived on confrontation; it was their lifeblood. Nick's problem was simply that he didn't understand their values. Personal relationships were private for Nick; for Laborde and McCormick, they were major stories, especially if one person was a diplomat and the other the widow of a star. It was just the sort of combination viewers would adore.

"This won't take very long, Mr. Manning," Laborde was insisting. "We just want a short interview. How long have you known Ella?"

"I'm not going to honor that question with a response," Nick stated flatly.

"Come on, Manning," McCormick broke in, inching forward. "It'll be a lot easier if you'll just tell us what's going on." His voice had assumed a quality of confidentiality, as if he were speaking man-to-man to an old friend. Nick resented it immediately.

"We just want to ask a few questions about Ella and Cody—" Laborde put in.

Nick became impatient. "Cody Butler has been dead for more than two years."

"You've been out of the country too long," Mc-Cormick told him. "Cody Butler is still big news. Ella knows that. Bring Ella out here."

"Then we'd better get some close shots," Laborde responded, signaling to the van where a cameraman emerged, his Minicam hoisted on his shoulder. Apparently, he'd been shooting the whole confrontation through the window of the van.

"Turn the camera off," Nick said quietly but firmly.

The cameraman responded to his order. Something about Nick's tone of voice obviously told the man he was serious.

"Keep on shooting," Laborde insisted. Because she'd shown some intimidation over the dogs, she seemed to want to prove herself, but she wasn't very effective; the cameraman didn't respond.

Nick took advantage of that reaction or lack of it to tell them all, "The interview is over. If you don't leave this property now, I'll let the dogs loose and *then* I'll call the police." His voice was calm, but there was no mistaking his seriousness.

As they backed off, McCormick said, "We'll just move the vans down to the end of the driveway. The street out there is public property, and we'll stay as long as it takes."

"Be my guest," Nick said. "Stay all night, or all week, for that matter. There's no story here." With that he turned on his heel and, still holding the dogs by their collars, went back into the house.

Ella had moved away from the window; she was visibly upset. "I'm so sorry," she began.

"You have nothing to be sorry about," Nick said. "It's my fault for not listening to you when you kept insisting this was going to happen. Well, now it's happened, and it's over."

"It's not over, Nick. It's just beginning. They're like vultures."

Nick laughed, but there was no mirth in the sound.

Ella walked to the window and looked out. "Where are they?"

"I told them to get off the property, so they're out on the street. It's a good quarter of a mile from here, Ella, and they can't see the house through the orchards."

"Thanks, Nick," she said, putting her arm around his waist and leaning her head on his shoulder. "You really handled them well."

"All the credit goes to the dogs. What do you suppose would have happened if I'd let them go?"

"They probably would have jumped up and licked the reporters in the face the way they do everyone else," she said, laughing.

"I expect you're right. Fortunately no one knew that." He joined in her laughter. "It's a good thing they didn't call my bluff. Look at them," he said, pointing to the dogs. One was asleep by the fire, unaware that the other one was nibbling at his ear. "Ferocious, aren't they?"

It was all over, and he and Ella were able to relax and laugh at what had happened. Nick pulled her down on the sofa next to him. "I don't like it, though. You have a right to go wherever you want with whomever you want, instead of living like a prisoner."

Ella knew what he was thinking; she was a prisoner at La Casa. She'd promised to get out into the world, and now it seemed to be her prison, also.

"There is a solution, Ella," he assured her. "We'll just have to continue to show the press that we mean business. Once they understand that and realize we're not news, they'll get bored and leave you alone."

At that moment, they heard the sound of motors revving up in the distance. Ella rushed to the window, and through the trees she could make out the lights of the two vans as they headed up the street toward the freeway entrance. "Well, *they* got bored very quickly," she said, looking back at Nick. "You got rid of them."

He joined her at the window and put his arm around her shoulder. "Maybe it's the beginning of the end for the press and Ella Butler," he suggested. "Now wasn't there a movie you wanted to watch on TV?"

They curled up on the sofa for the next two hours, the dogs at their feet, and watched a forties movie, a sentimental romance that left Ella crying tears of happiness at the end. "I get right into these old movies," she told him. "You need to know that about me."

"Just another one of your lovable traits," he said. As he got up to turn off the television set, his own face came on the screen.

"Oh, no," Ella said dully.

In horrified silence they watched the tape of Nick's confrontation with the reporters, carefully edited down to his threats with the dogs.

"I don't believe it," Ella said as the tape ended. "They had no story."

"Wait a minute," Nick answered, silencing her to watch the rest of the news segment. The anchorman was talking about Cody, his death, the continuing worship of his fans, and suddenly there was another tape, this one of Ella at the funeral. "What in the world—" Nick began.

Ella took the initiative then, striding over to the TV and turning it off. "They always roll that tape when there's a story about me or Cody."

"Ella," he said with pain in his voice, "how terrible for you."

"I'm immune to it. At least that wasn't network TV," she added, searching for something positive, "and they didn't divulge where we are. Maybe the networks won't pick up on it."

"I'm sure they won't. It's over, and they've had their day. We just won't think about it anymore," he promised himself and her.

When they went to bed, they didn't make love. Nick just held her close until she fell asleep peacefully in his arms.

The peace that had comforted her into sleep stayed with her through the night, and Ella woke refreshed, still in Nick's arms.

"Feel better?" he asked softly, his lips caressing her cheek as he spoke.

"I feel wonderful," Ella said. The incident of the previous night seemed unimportant to her this morning. They were together, and it was the last day of their long weekend. Ella wanted to make the most of it. She gave him a quick kiss on the cheek and bounded out of bed.

"I'm going to make breakfast for you."

"Coffee and orange juice?" he asked.

"Nope. Grits, ham, fried eggs *and* coffee and orange juice. I bought everything at the store the other day."

"Even a ham?"

"Well, I bought slices in the deli section. I'll fry it with the eggs. Very tasty and very fattening," she admitted. "But first a shower. Are you joining me?" She gave him a provocative look that got Nick right out of bed.

"I don't know when I've ever had a better invitation," he said.

"How about the time you were invited to the White House for dinner with all those diplomats and their wives?"

"I've been there several times," Nick corrected. "I've also met the Queen at Buckingham Palace and had an audience with the Pope in the Vatican. Ask me how this compares." He put his arms around her.

"Well, you can't really compare state occasions with something like this."

"Oh, yes you can," he whispered, blowing softly in her ear. "And they pale beside it."

"How about all those dates with Washington socialites?"

"Not even in the same ballpark," he said, kissing the gentle curve of her neck.

Ella felt herself melting into him. "How about..." she began.

She didn't get to finish her sentence. The persistent knocking on the door and ringing of the bell finally got through to them. They didn't know how long it had been going on, but now there was no ignoring it. The sigh that escaped Ella's lips was one of resignation; it was as if she'd known all along this would happen and had just willed herself into believing differently, maybe for Nick's sake, maybe for the sake of them both.

They went over to the window and looked out. There were cars and vans lining the drive.

"I wonder why the dogs didn't bark," Nick said almost to himself.

"I think they did," Ella said. "We just didn't hear them. They're certainly barking now." She looked down into the driveway, naming for Nick the reporters as they got out of their cars.

"Any network people?"

"No, I don't think so. These are all from the scandal sheets."

"They don't matter," he offered.

"No, they don't, but they're still trouble, because they print anything and everything, often whether it's true or not. Once when I had intestinal flu, they speculated that I was recovering from a drug overdose," Ella remembered. "Another paper picked up on it, and pretty soon they had me in a drug rehab. No," she agreed, "they don't matter to us, but they don't ever go away."

"Someday they will," he promised, but he'd made other promises; they both remembered. He could no longer pretend everything was fine. His face had been on local television; before long it might hit the networks. In the meantime, there were reporters all over, swarming like bees in the orchards. Something had to be done.

"I'd better call Art," Ella said, going to the phone.

"No."

"Please, Nick. He can come here with an escort, guards—"

"We don't need guards, Ella. This isn't a war zone."

"Then what'll we do?" Her voice was frantic.

"I'll get rid of them, just like before." He started pulling on his clothes.

"I'm sorry, Nick."

"As I already told you, Ella; it's not your fault."

"Not directly, but if it weren't for who I am—or was—no one would even care. At least this has been a lesson for you." She, too, had begun to dress.

He looked at her questioningly.

"You can't be with me and keep your privacy. This certainly isn't going to go down well with the State Department. Your career—"

"I don't care about my career. It's not my whole life. Maybe for Cody it was, but not for me."

"Is it Cody you really blame for all this?"

"I guess I do, in a way. He was responsible for much of that publicity, Ella. When a celebrity travels in a stretch limo with a huge entourage, people notice. I've been around the rich and privileged all my life, and there's a way to stay out of the limelight, a way to behave."

"Your way? The Manning way, I suppose," she said sharply. Ella could feel her head throbbing; she hadn't meant to argue, but his words had reminded her of the difference between them. "I suppose no one at La Casa had that kind of class."

"Stop that," he ordered her, "right now. We aren't going to let this circus come between us. We're going to take it out on them, not on each other." He nodded toward the window.

Ella sighed deeply, walked over and pulled back the curtain. She'd finished dressing and was ready for the next move, whatever that might be, when she looked down and saw Art making his way through the bevy of reporters to the front door.

"There's Art," she said.

"How did he—"

"I don't know," Ella said, "but I'd better let him in." She rushed past Nick and down the stairs. He followed her. When she turned toward him just before she opened the door to let Art in, she saw the look of anger on his face. She'd rushed off without a word from Nick, gone to let Art in as if he were their savior.

Apparently, as far as Art was concerned, that was exactly the case.

"You should tell me when you do these things, Ella," Art said as he slipped in through the door and closed it behind him, shutting out the din.

"I don't believe it's necessary for Ella to clear her weekends with you," Nick answered for her. "How did you find out where we were?"

"That's not important," Art answered curtly. "We have to get Ella out of here. Is there a back approach to this place?"

"Just a minute," Nick said, stepping between Art and Ella. "We didn't ask you to come here, and we don't need your assistance."

Nick's anger was boiling over now, not just at Art but at the reporters outside and the whole ridiculous situation. It was happening again; Ella's notoriety was getting in the way of their romance.

"Listen," he said, trying to modulate his voice. "We aren't the settlers being attacked by Indians, and you certainly aren't the cavalry. Ella and I can get ourselves out of this."

"Now, you listen," Art said, gesturing with his ever-present cigarette. "Those reporters out there are worse than any Indians you've ever heard of. They'd love to drag your name and Ella's through the dirt. Frankly, I don't care what happens to you, but I sure as hell am not going to let anything happen to Ella. You've already been on TV—"

"It was only local," Ella broke in.

"Honey, news travels fast, especially when it concerns Cody Butler's widow shacking up with some guy. It'll be network by tomorrow."

At that, Nick stepped forward and reached for Art. Ella managed to slip between them and grab Nick's arm.

"Nick, please. No fighting. I can't take that on top of everything else. Let's try to concentrate on outsmarting the army of reporters outside."

The muscle in Nick's jaw tautened, and for a moment Ella thought he was going to brush aside her restraining arm and go for Art. By the look on Art's face, he thought so, too. There was real fear in his pale blue eyes. Then abruptly Nick turned away and said, "You're right, Ella. We've got enough problems. The man who loves you wants to beat the hell out of your buddy here, but the diplomat in me says discretion is the better part of valor. At least for today."

Within half an hour they were packed and leaving Yorba Linda in separate cars. As Nick glanced at Ella when her car headed down the narrow back road to the street, he thought she looked trapped. In a way she was. Her dream had faded. Art was in control again.

Chapter 8

Still in her robe, Ella walked down the hall at La Casa to her office. The door was open, and Nikki sat at the desk, typing. For a moment Ella forgot all about the events of the previous day and lingered in the doorway, watching her secretary and friend at the typewriter. Nikki had a special style that Ella suspected was unequaled in the clerical world. Her fingers were always on the wrong keys, but somehow she managed to come up with the right letters, and did so in record time.

"Maybe you should publish your own typing manual," Ella said, greeting Nikki with a hug.

"Not possible. I have no idea *how* I do it." She pulled a page from the machine. "Here's a letter to the fan clubs. I think it can be printed up and sent to all of them during Cody's birthday celebration. It's generic enough, and Lord knows you don't want to have to write a different letter to every club.''

"You're right about that," Ella said, plopping down in a wicker chair and glancing over the letter. "This seems fine." She handed it back to Nikki and looked at her with an expression that was quizzical and scolding at the same time. "What are you hiding, Nikki?"

"Me?" Nikki answered innocently.

"What's under the stack of papers that you so quickly rearranged?"

"Just something that we probably should get to later," Nikki answered casually.

"No, let's tackle it now."

"Ella, it's awfully early, and quite frankly you look terrible. There's nothing here that can't wait until later in the day. After a few more letters, a couple of calls—"

"What else?" Ella had a feeling she knew the answer.

Nikki still avoided it. "Did you sleep at all last night?"

"Not much. I assume Art told you what happened."

Nikki nodded. "He called yesterday after you all got back. I wanted to come over, but he said you were resting."

"Those were his orders to me," Ella said. "Actually, I swam for an hour and then watched an old movie in the projection room and tried not to think about the disarray of my life. Which is probably documented somewhere under that stack of papers. Surely the scandal sheets aren't out already?"

Nikki sighed. "Actually, you just managed to get into one at the eleventh hour when the presses were about to roll."

"What luck," Ella said bitterly. "Let me see it."

Reluctantly, Nikki pulled one of the most lurid of all the scandal sheets out from under the stack and handed it to Ella. "I *would* make the *Whisper*, my favorite." She laughed ruefully as she read the bold headline: "Diplomat and Cody's Widow Caught in Love Tryst." Beneath was a photo of Ella and Nick emerging from the house in Yorba Linda. Ella's face was hidden; Nick's was twisted and angry.

Ella spoke quietly, matter-of-factly to Nikki. "Art warned us not to go outside together, but Nick insisted on putting me in one car before he went off in the other one. I guess Art was right," she added as she looked at the picture of two people she hardly recognized; they didn't look anything like the happy lovers who had spent such a perfect weekend together.

"There are more pictures inside," Nikki told her. "It gets worse."

Ella opened the paper to the photo spread on the next page.

"They didn't have much to say. I suppose the motto is: No copy, use old photos," Nikki commented.

"Where in the world did they get this?" Ella had glanced at the usual pictures of her and Cody, Cody in performance, the crowds at his funeral, until her eye was caught by one at the bottom of the page. It was a huge house on a sloping lawn with horses grazing behind a fence in the distance. "Fox Haven," she said, "I've never even seen it."

"What do they call it? 'Diplomat's Ancestral Home'? The archives at that gossip rag must be enormous," she added. "Can you imagine? Drawers filled with photographs of the homes of people in government, the arts, business, everyone who might conceivably be news someday. It boggles the mind."

"Either that or they whisked a photographer off to Virginia last night to take shots of the house and wire them back here."

Ella and Nikki continued to speculate on the tactics of the *Whisper* as Ella read over the other brief stories, including one about the possibility of Cody's reaction beyond the grave. The idea was so crazy that it was almost funny. Before long they were giggling about the absurdity of the whole situation and the paper's ability to make big news from such a slim premise.

"You and Cody used to laugh about those kinds of stories," Nikki reminded her.

"Yes, we did, but sometimes I think Cody really liked reading about himself in the scandal sheets, even when the facts were wrong."

"Cody was a star. He didn't shy away from publicity," Nikki said.

"On the other hand, Nick won't be thrilled to see this."

"Will he be terribly upset?"

Ella thought for a moment. "I would have said *yes* if you'd asked me that question a couple of days ago, but we were also on television."

"So Art told me."

"Nick didn't seem bothered about it at all, but he may have been trying to hide his concern from me.

Whatever the reaction, his superiors at the State Department are probably seeing red, to say nothing of his parents."

Nikki handed her a message slip. "He called earlier and left a number where you can reach him tonight. He's going down to Virginia."

"To Fox Haven," Ella said. "Possibly to face his parents and try to justify his relationship with me—or maybe even explain me away."

"I doubt that," Nikki said.

"Had he seen this?" Ella asked, thumping the paper in her lap.

"Didn't mention it. Just said for you to please call him tonight."

Ella suddenly felt a little shaky. "I'm not sure I'm ready to talk to him yet."

"Ella, don't be silly. We were just laughing over this ridiculous publicity a few minutes ago. No one takes those rags seriously; certainly Nick's parents won't."

Ella nodded, but she didn't feel the least bit convinced. "Maybe we should get some work done."

"Good idea. Oh, we just got a telex from the Dunnes this morning. They've gone through the old villa, and the prospects for remodeling are perfect; they're putting together a proposal for the clinic."

"I knew they'd be successful," Ella said. "It's going to work, Nikki."

"I know, and I'm very excited."

Ella leaned back in her chair thoughtfully. "Once the clinic's an accomplished fact, operating with a competent staff to take care of the islanders, I'll feel damned good."

"That'll be your first big step toward getting free of all this." Nikki's gesture included La Casa, the fans waiting outside the gate and all they represented.

"The next step will be *complete* freedom, moving out of the house."

"You can do it," Nikki said encouragingly.

"I used to think La Casa was my protection, but now I know it's my jail." Ella added, "If only there were real freedom outside... But since there's not, I'll just have to get out there and face whatever awaits me. Nick's given me the incentive to go for it, but his involvement could wreak havoc on his career."

"Nick's a big boy, Ella. He knew what he was getting into," Nikki reminded her.

"No, he didn't," Ella argued. "He didn't realize what could happen, but he found out soon enough after a day at La Casa and a weekend in Yorba Linda. It was a mistake to think of our idyll continuing outside of paradise, but we couldn't stay on Balboa forever, could we?"

The question hung in the air, unanswered, as a knock sounded on the open door. Art Newcombe stepped into the room and tossed a bunch of newspapers onto the desk. There was an unpleasant look on his face. The cigarette in the corner of his mouth was unlit. He was clearly preoccupied.

"Besides the scandal sheets, we also made the dailies." He reached down, picked up the newspaper on top and opened it. Not waiting for a response to his abrupt entrance, he began to read from one of the popular Los Angeles gossip columns: "'It looks like Ella Butler's fans are feeling a little disappointed in her today. Seems she was discovered with her lover at a hideaway in North Orange County. Well, it had to happen, folks. Ella had to find another man eventually, but the discouraging part comes when we find out who he is: not an exciting new star, not even an eccentric millionaire. Just another guy. A little drab, it seems to us. He has something to do with the government. Cody wouldn't be very impressed.' "

"On the other hand," Art continued, reaching for another paper.

"Art, enough is enough," Nikki suggested.

"You gotta hear this one, because the theory is different. They call Nick a 'Hot Shot Diplomat.' But any way you slice it, Ella, it's not good."

Nikki made a little noise in her throat and then couldn't control herself. "This is ridiculous, Art. Ella deserves a life of her own. She's entitled to it by now."

"I know Ella's entitled, Nikki, but understand my concern. People, lots of people, still care about Cody and those around him. He's a legend, and we need to protect that. He's like a god to them, and Ella's like—"

"Please, Art, don't finish that sentence," Nikki begged.

"Well, she's special to them."

"I can't go on being an appendage of Cody, Art," Ella spoke up.

"I'm not asking that, baby, but what you do affects the memory of him. We've got the retrospective album coming out next month. All this negative stuff can't help us, Ella. Not good for the corporate image."

Nikki got up, slammed a file on the desk and stalked past Art, turning as she got to the doorway. "I can't take any more of this. I'm going downstairs for a cup of coffee with Juanita until Art finishes his spiel.''

"It's not a spiel, Nikki, and you know it," Art rebuked her. "Cody was good to Ella. He loved her and he gave her a great life."

"Which means she owes the rest of it to him?" Nikki asked sarcastically.

"Course not," Art replied, "but she owes the fans some respect, darling."

"Don't darling me, Art. I'm not in the mood."

"Okay, then go have your coffee. This is between Ella and me, anyway."

"You bet it is," Nikki answered as she went out the door and closed it behind her.

"Ella—" Art began.

"I don't want to do anything to reflect badly on Cody's memory, Art. You know that. I'm indebted to him for his love, but I showed that while he was alive. I protected his image then, and I forgave him a great deal."

She watched as Art nodded understandingly. He'd been there at the end when Cody was having drinking problems, drinking and barely avoiding big trouble; in fact, Art had been the one who'd kept him out of trouble. Ella had been the one who'd forgiven him. Together they'd maintained his image. Ella had been grateful to Art then, and now she was returning the favor by helping him preserve the image. But enough was enough, she thought.

"Damn it, Art, I need a life of my own," she cried.

"A life with Manning, you mean."

"No, I mean *on my own*. This isn't about Manning; it's about me."

"You have a life here, Ella. Everything you want or need is at La Casa."

"Not everything. Only this room is mine. I want a place of my own."

"You'd leave La Casa? You couldn't, you wouldn't..." He was sputtering in disbelief. "If you could only see what's going on outside. Just now, when I came in, there were fans all over the place, some of them carrying signs like 'Stay true to Cody, Ella' or 'Don't betray him.'"

Ella didn't know whether she believed that or not, but she knew the fans were there, this morning as always. "I don't know what I'm going to do after I get through this mess, but moving out of La Casa is an option, one I'm going to think about."

Art's face wore a look of grave concern; the paleness had turned to pallor. "Everything will calm down," he assured her, "and you'll feel better, but you have to hold on to La Casa; it's part of him."

"We'll see, Art." Ella felt very cruel as she spoke, knowing what her words were doing to Art, well aware that his life was nothing without Cody's memory to sustain him. It was true; Art had lived for Cody and would continue to live for him. He had no wife or family of his own; he'd never wanted that. He'd gotten wealth and a certain kind of fame at Cody's side, and yet Ella knew it was no longer the attention or even the money that Art needed. He needed to keep Cody's flame burning, and Ella was threatening to put it out.

"I'd never do anything to reflect badly on Cody," she assured Art again, "but when the time comes, I'm going to step out of the limelight. The fans will still have Cody. They don't need me, too."

James Nicholas Manning Jr. stood with one elbow resting on the marble mantelpiece in the library of Fox Haven. His long, narrow face was thoughtful as he paused in conversation with his son before asking, "What do the people at State say about all the recent publicity, Son?"

Nick was stretched out in a floral club chair, his feet on the matching ottoman. His expression was relaxed, not at all worried. He glanced over at his mother with a smile before answering. Grace was the one who was most concerned; she was the one to placate.

"I spent most of the day with Gavin, who had talked to the Secretary. I suppose to say they weren't pleased would be something of an understatement."

"So I would think," his father responded. "Of course, you were no more than a victim of circumstance."

"I wish I could agree, J.N.," Nick answered, then took a sip of his drink. Like everyone else, including his mother, Nick had always addressed the elder Manning by his initials. That seemed more appropriate than James or Jim, certainly more so than Father. Although he was a good family man, a stern disciplinarian and role model, J. N. Manning had never thought of himself as a father type.

"Surely you weren't responsible for the actions of the press," J.N. said, making a statement rather than asking a question.

"I created some of the problem by confronting them."

"You've handled the press all your life." Nick's mother came to her son's defense.

"Yes, Mother, but the so-called newsmen who hang around celebrities are vultures, not reporters."

J.N. seemed impatient with the direction the conversation was taking. "Press aside, what's all this rubbish going to do to your chance of an ambassadorship?" He walked over to the bar and poured himself a drink under the watchful eye of his wife. After a serious heart attack followed by triple bypass surgery, J. N. Manning still liked his bourbon.

"They're keeping it very low-key, actually."

"Hmm," came the response. J.N. had always planned for his son to follow in his footsteps. Nick knew that what he did in his spare time was of no interest to his father as long as it didn't affect his career adversely.

"For the time being, according to Gavin, they have a temporary assignment for me, visiting some of the small one-man posts throughout the world and evaluating their effectiveness."

"That sounds interesting," his father commented. "Give you a chance to ride out this wave of bad publicity."

"It was a one-time thing, wasn't it, Son?" Grace's look told Nick that she expected an affirmative response.

Nick laughed. "Don't worry, Mother. I have no desire to tangle with the press again, and if you wonder, I didn't resort to violence."

"Why, I'm sure you didn't, Son."

"Yes, an assignment such as the one Gavin has in mind could be very helpful," J.N. mused, ignoring the discussion of his son's *contretemps* with the press.

Grace, however, worried less about politics than about personal relationships. That had always been the case, and Nick braced himself for the question that was forming on her lips. "Will you be seeing..." She paused as if struggling for a way to refer to Ella. "Will you see Mrs. Butler again?"

"I hope so," Nick answered. "I've been waiting for her to call." He glanced at his watch and wondered why he hadn't heard from Ella.

"I'm sure all of this must be difficult for her." She added what to Nick was a less-than-subtle put-down. "Of course, those kinds of people are used to being in the public eye."

"What kinds of people, Mother?"

"Did Gavin say when this new assignment would begin?" J.N. said, interrupting. He'd successfully managed to avoid the tack his wife was taking and go on to what he considered the crux of the matter. Nick was used to that; his parents often carried on two different conversations with the same person. He smiled to himself. They often carried on two different conversations with *each other*.

"As soon as they can get the ball rolling I should be back at work," Nick answered his father. "Of course, you know what that means at State."

J.N. chuckled. "I do indeed, Son. I was there not so long ago myself, if you remember."

"Her kind of people are the ones who are in the limelight." Oblivious to her husband, Grace had come up with a polite way of referring to Ella. "Celebrities," she added.

Nick smiled at his mother. "Her husband was a celebrity, Mother. Ella doesn't automatically take on that title just because she was married to him."

"Well..." Grace began.

"She's a very private person," Nick defended Ella. "You'd like her."

The silence lasted a little too long. Finally Grace answered, "I'm sure I would, Son." Then as if to placate Nick, she reminded her husband that they had once seen Cody Butler in concert. "A few years ago, at a fund-raiser in New York. It was for the World's Children, I believe, J.N. Do you remember? He was quite a *dynamic* young man," she said, searching for an inoffensive word but unable to come up with one that flattered.

"Hmm," J.N. replied, "I do remember that. The tickets were three hundred dollars, and the music was unconscionably loud."

"Not just the music," Grace said, remembering. "His fans were very vocal."

"They still are," Nick said, thinking about the crowds outside La Casa.

"I'm surprised that she remains so much a part of that life. She must be attracted to it in some way."

"It's complicated," Nick answered, but he understood what his mother was saying. He was also irritated at Ella for not being able to break away. At the same time, he'd seen the pressure she was facing, the publicity she had to deal with. It wasn't easy for her, and his own idea that she could just walk away from it by walking away from La Casa had proven both right and wrong. They'd had three wonderful days in Yorba Linda, not even being noticed. Then they'd had the confrontation that had ended in their being whisked off in opposite directions.

Nick refused his father's offer of another drink and looked at his watch again, wondering why Ella hadn't called. He had no doubt Nikki had given her the message. Nikki was his biggest supporter. It had been obvious to Nick all along that she would be happy to see her friend get out from under the shadow of Cody Butler.

Deciding to call Ella again, Nick swung his feet off the ottoman and started to get up when a maid appeared at the library door. Dinner was served. Nick sighed and took his mother's arm. After dinner, if she still hadn't called, he'd try again.

J.N. walked toward the dining room on the other side of his wife, his tall, slim physique a contrast to her pleasantly plump one. He patted her hand affectionately, and Nick smiled to himself. His parents were quite a duo, totally opposite, often not even aware of each other. It was an unusual marriage that had worked for more than forty years. It was right for them, but Nick's marriage would be different. He and Ella... He stopped in midthought. A future with Ella was far from a certainty.

"How about a game of billiards after dinner?" J.N. asked his son as they sat down at the table.

"That'd be fine, J.N." was the answer. Then, after the game, if she still hadn't called ...

*   *   *

Twilight was falling at La Casa. Nikki and Art had left. Juanita had brought Ella a tray in her room. The house was quiet and very lonely.

Ella pushed away her half-eaten meal, looked at the phone and then at Nick's number on the pink message slip. She should call him; Ella knew that. But she didn't know what to say. *This isn't working out? This will never work out?* Rationality told her she was right. The furor over the diplomat and Cody's widow wouldn't die down in a week or even a month. It would grow and fester, and it could ruin Nick's career.

He would argue, say that it wasn't true, but he would be wrong. There wasn't a future for them yet. Maybe someday, when she left La Casa and established her own life, when the fans finally drifted away, maybe then there'd be a time and a place for them. Ella loved him, she realized now that they were apart, and the feeling for him had intensified. He loved her; of that she was certain, but love wouldn't be enough to get them through.

The sharp ring of the phone made Ella jump. She reached over and picked up the receiver.

"Ella," Nick said coolly. "I've been waiting for you to call."

"I was going to, but—"

"Were you?" he asked almost bitterly. "I don't think so, somehow. In fact, I think you had no intention of calling."

"Of course I did, Nick. I—"

"Were you planning to walk out of my life? Disappear?" He said that lightly, to offset the bitter tone that had insinuated itself into his voice, but he was still anxious. He couldn't hide that.

"Of course not," she answered, "but after what happened in Yorba Linda, I'm surprised you want to see me. I've brought a lot of problems into your life, Nick."

"You're never a problem, Ella."

"I'm surrounded by them, though."

He laughed. "Yes, that's true, but I'm the kind of person who thrives on problems. I can fix them, Ella," he assured her.

"I wish I could believe they were fixable," she said sadly.

"They are. I'll prove that next time. We'll plan everything more carefully."

"I'm tired of being careful, tired of running and hiding. I want to see you," she admitted, "but—"

"That's what I want, too," he said, interrupting before she could explain. "It's what I need." There was a catch in his voice, and suddenly Ella could see him, his dark hair falling across his forehead, his intense eyes, the set of his jaw when he was serious, as he was now. She felt a tremble go through her as he spoke.

"I need to wake up next to you and hold you close. I need to make love to you in the night."

"Nick, please," she begged. It wasn't fair of him to recall what it was like when they were together.

"What is it, Ella?"

"It can't be like that for us until my life settles down. What you're describing is paradise, and paradise is only on Balboa."

"No, Ella, it's anywhere we're together."

"Not if the press is there, Nick. I don't want to go through that again, and I certainly don't want you to go through it. You have your future, your career. Another skirmish like that and you might just have to forget about the State Department."

"You don't need to worry yourself about that, Ella."

"But I do worry, and for a good reason." Ella knew Nick was jeopardizing his career to be with her, and he wouldn't even admit it to himself. She had to convince him that each time they were together would be bad for him, worse than the time before. If he couldn't be convinced—and Ella was afraid that he couldn't—then the next step was up to her.

"It's time for me to find some direction, Nick, maybe even move out of La Casa."

"I've thought that was a good idea all along," he agreed. "Why don't you consider coming here, to D.C. or Virginia? We could be together, and I could help you through the transition."

Ella gripped the phone tightly. That wasn't what she meant. She tried to explain without sounding ungrateful. "That would be like going from one hiding place to another. I need to be on my own. I need time—"

"I may not have the time, Ella. I've waited thirty-seven years to find you; *now's* the time for us."

"Did you see the papers, Nick?" she asked suddenly.

"No," he answered.

"You will," she assured him, "and so will your people at State, and they're not going to like what they see. Another episode like this could ruin you, Nick. That's why we have to go slowly.''

"I don't care about the papers.'' His voice was sharp. "Slowly is not my pace.''

"What we have for each other will last, Nick. If you can just wait a little longer.''

"I have no plans to wait,'' he said brusquely.

"That sounds like an ultimatum.''

"I suppose it is,'' he answered.

"Nick—''

The line went dead. Shakily, Ella hung up. She hardly knew what they'd said, why the call had ended so abruptly. She only knew that she couldn't allow him to risk his future in another encounter with the press. Eventually, she'd be on her feet, away from the ghostly presence of Cody and the very real presence of Art. They'd *have* to wait.

The slide on the screen was a surprise to Ella. "I never saw the villa up close when I was in Kikao. It's lovely.''

"And it's just the place to set up the clinic,'' Doug said. "You were right about that. It was built years ago for a vacation home and rarely used. Even though it's been deserted for a while, it's not in bad shape.''

"It's perfect,'' Ella said.

"I think so,'' Susan Dunne responded as her husband flipped to the next slide. "This is the downstairs interior. We can put the examining rooms here. The plumbing is adequate, and it won't be too difficult to add a sink in each room.''

Ella watched the screen as the Dunnes went through their stack of slides, explaining the remodeling that would be required to turn the old villa into an adequate medical facility.

"I imagine hiring workers won't be a problem," Ella said as Doug turned the lights in the office back on.

"No problem at all," he replied. "Manpower is certainly available in the islands. After all, they built that whole resort with a small construction team supervising. All the supervision we need is an architect and a builder."

"If we tempt them with the beauty of the setting, we can probably get the price down considerably."

"My thoughts exactly," Doug said with a smile. "I happen to know a couple of guys who are overdue for a vacation."

"Then let's get things rolling, Doug," Ella said. "I'll plan a meeting with my lawyer and the accountant tomorrow. I'd like for you both to be there to give them some numbers to begin with. When we get firm bids, we can earmark the funds. Is it too early to begin interviewing a staff?"

Doug sat back in his chair and lit his pipe. "Not at all," he said. "We'd like to supervise."

"The hiring?" Ella asked. "I'd always assumed you would."

"No, Ella," Susan put in. "We want to supervise the clinic."

Ella stared at Susan, her jaw dropping. "What about your jobs here at the hospital?"

"We can take a leave of absence. I've already broached the subject with the chief of staff. I didn't want to go into details until I'd talked with you."

"Well, I'd be thrilled, obviously," Ella said. "When did you two get this idea?"

"We've been discussing it ever since we saw the villa. With every day that passed as we put together the proposal, it began to look more like a viable possibility for us. We have no family, no kids. It would be a challenge as well as an opportunity to change our lifestyle."

"We've never considered southern California a permanent stop," Susan added.

"Well, I'm ecstatic," Ella said. "I couldn't think of a better solution than putting the clinic in the hands of the doctors Dunne. Let's go over the details and get everything settled now."

By the time Doug had left his office to make the afternoon rounds, the plans were under way, and Ella's spirits were high. But Susan stopped as they went out the door and put a hand on Ella's arm.

"What's the matter?" she asked.

"Why, nothing," Ella responded. "I've never been so excited. It's all moving so fast—"

"That's not what I mean," Susan said. "You look awful, Ella, in spite of your excitement over the clinic. When Doug turned on the lights after the slide show, I'm sure I saw tears in your eyes."

"Just memory tears," Ella said evasively. "I had a lovely time in the islands."

"Is it over?"

Ella walked back into the room and sat down, ready to talk to Susan. "I'm not sure," she admitted. "Being together hasn't worked out very well for Nick and me. I thought it would help if we could wait until I broke away from La Casa and all it represents, and maybe then everything would change.''

"I'm sure you're right, and you've already begun to break away with the clinic.''

"He's not a patient man,'' Ella said with a smile at the understatement. "He's rushing me. I feel like a rag doll, being pulled one way by him and another by Art. On the phone last week Nick and I had a very unsatisfying conversation. I'm not even sure how it ended, and I kept thinking he'd call back, but he never did. Then Art appeared this morning. Just when I'm ready to begin the break, I find he's made arrangements for me to go to Baltimore on a public appearance.''

"Why didn't you refuse?'' Susan asked.

"This one is special, a ground-breaking for a new cancer center. The Cody Butler Foundation gave the seed money, and the rest was raised by donations.''

"That happens fairly often,'' Susan said.

"I know, but in this case, children raised some of the money with school projects. It was hard work, and it paid off. I feel obligated to go and thank them, but this is the last time. I tried to make Art aware of that this morning.'' Ella gave a little sigh. "I don't think he believes me, and I can understand why. My threats are never carried out.''

"This time will be different,'' Susan assured her. "By the way, isn't Nick in Washington, D.C., much of the time?''

"Yes,'' Ella said.

"And isn't Baltimore very close to Washington?'' There was a sparkle in her eyes.

"It is, but I'm not going to see him.''

At Susan's puzzled look, Ella said quietly, "Nick has made it very clear that he doesn't approve of my involvement in Cody's legacy. I don't think this is the time for Nick and me to work out our problems." She said nothing about the press, but she knew they'd be there in full force. No, this trip was for Cody, her swan song.

Chapter 9

Despite the disagreement she'd had with Art over the trip, Ella was glad she'd come. The events surrounding the opening of the Cancer Research Center of Baltimore had been well planned. She'd met with the board of trustees in the morning and had been guest of honor at a luncheon that afternoon. The news people covering the events had been attentive, asking questions with no reference to Ella's private life. She'd appreciated that, but the best part of the day came at three o'clock as the school bell rang across the street from the center.

All of the kids came pouring out of their classrooms onto the playground, where they gathered to greet Ella. Through their own projects, with very little teacher assistance, they'd raised money for the center, and Ella had insisted they be present when she cut the ribbon.

What happened next wasn't on the agenda. It was spontaneous. Gathering around Ella in a big circle, the kids raised their voices in Cody's theme song, "Where My Heart Is." As they sang the familiar words, Ella felt tears well up in her eyes. It was a lovely day in late April; the trees along the avenue were blossoming bright pink. Ella, too, was in pink, feeling as vital and alive as the awakening spring around her. The sky was bright and clear; a slight breeze stirred as the song came to an end. The children on the inner circle nearest Ella gave her a big hug and joined hands to walk with her across the street where the dignitaries waited for the ribbon-cutting ceremony.

The rest of the day proceeded as planned, and by the time it ended, Ella was both pleased and relieved. It had gone well. More important, it was over. Over for good. This would be her last appearance as Ella Butler, Cody's widow. His foundation would continue to support such projects, but Ella would no longer participate. No one was aware of that except Art, and he still refused to believe it. But the happiness that engulfed her was more than what it seemed, a reaction to spring, the children and the center. Only she knew that it was also a reaction to the new life that awaited her.

She smiled, the dignitaries clapped, the children cheered, and Ella felt her spirits soar. She hoped that someday in the future, when she stood alone, firmly on her own feet, Nick would be there with her, but whatever happened, this was the beginning. She'd never felt so free.

"Mrs. Butler, your limousine's here," one of the organizers said, slipping through the crowd to Ella's side. "If you'll just follow me."

The limo waited at the corner, no more than fifty feet away, but those fifty feet, the last she would walk as Cody's widow, were peppered with reporters. Not the press members who'd covered the event, but scavengers, the ones Ella had been prepared to see. Apparently, they'd found out about the ceremony and come to Baltimore with their usual haste and usual questions.

"Are you going to stop in D.C.?" one of them asked as she approached the limo.

"Is it still on between you and Nick Manning?" came the next question.

"We heard it was all over," another called out.

Ella neither answered the questions nor commented on the observations. With eyes straight ahead and the perplexed young man who'd been her guide for the day still by her side, she made her way through the throng and ducked into the waiting car. The young man closed the door after her with a quick handshake and mumbled thanks and then moved out of the way as the car sped off.

"Straight to the airport, please," Ella said, leaning forward to speak into the intercom.

"The driver already has his instructions."

Ella whirled around to see Nick beside her in the dark interior of the car. Her emotions bounded all over the place from joy to irritation and then to relief. She'd had no intention of seeing him on this trip; in fact, she'd planned her arrival and departure precisely to allow no extra time for Nick. Obviously, he'd had other ideas.

"How did you get the limo?" she asked, more startled than angry but still trying to define all of her other feelings.

"Commandeered it," he said simply, as if that were a usual occurrence for him.

Before Ella could answer, Nick had taken her in his arms. The curtain between the front and the rest of the car was drawn, hiding them from the driver's sight, and the glass partition effectively cut off all sound. The windows were tinted against the outside sun, and the lights throughout the car had been dimmed. Nick reached for a button that turned them off completely just as his lips found Ella's.

She meant to protest, but it was already too late. Everything she'd felt for him since that moment their eyes first met on the boat to Kikao she felt now, more intensely. The reporters who were probably following the limo were forgotten. Forgotten, too, was her plan to run for the safety of the airplane back to California. Ella had no idea where they were going, and at this moment she didn't care. She'd told herself she could do everything without him, but there was one problem with that: she couldn't *live* without him.

"Ella," he said softly, his lips touching her ear, nibbling, licking at the lobe between whispers of her name. "Oh, Ella, Ella." He hadn't had any definite plan in mind except to whisk her away with him to Virginia. Now he saw clearly what was going to happen, and there was no stopping it. They'd been apart too long. Even a day was too long. She'd been on his mind and in his heart, and now he was holding her close and the love he felt was turning his veins to fire.

He gently nibbled the soft flesh just below her earlobe and heard her sharp intake of breath and felt her arms tighten around him. She wanted what he wanted, and she wanted it now. With relief, he found her lips again and kissed her powerfully, pulling her over on top of him on the wide seat.

Nick hadn't known that this was going to happen, so he hadn't stopped to consider her reaction. If he had, he might have thought it would be shy and unresponsive. She wasn't the type to react so spontaneously, almost fiercely. Yet that's just what was happening. Her hands clasped around his neck, holding him closer and closer as his tongue plunged into her mouth and his lips ravaged her sweetness. She tasted of springtime, and he wondered if he would be able to get enough of her.

There seemed to be a force compelling him to kiss her deeper and deeper, hold her tighter and tighter, a force he couldn't resist. He found the zipper on her pink dress and pulled at it urgently. It caught in the material and he cursed under his breath, but Ella had moved around beside him until he was able to slide his hands down the dress to its hem and push it upward, over her thighs and stomach to her waist.

Ella helped him peel off her panty hose as she wiggled back into place beside him. Then he felt her hands at his belt, unbuckling it and, with more deftness than he'd been able to manage, unzipping his trousers and reaching for him with loving fingers. He tried to say her name again, but the word didn't form. His mouth was on hers; his fingers were moving down to touch her honeyed moistness as she stroked and then guided him until he felt the shaft of his desire touch that feathery place, press against her and, with her fingers still guiding, slip into her.

It was all so sweet and easy Nick could hardly believe it. With a deep sigh he rolled over until he was on top and Ella's legs were wrapped around him. Their lips were still joined. At no time had the kiss been interrupted. Now as he moved deep within her he could control himself no longer. The sweetness had ended. Burying his hand in her thick hair, he kissed her with such force that he thought she might cry out. She didn't. She kissed him back, as they moved faster and faster. Each time Nick plunged into her Ella received him with welcoming passion.

Just when Nick thought the moment had come for both of them, he managed to pause and lift himself up onto his elbows, for the first time taking his mouth from hers. In the near darkness he could see her eyes shining as they looked deeply into his; he could see the hint of a smile on her face. Their shared eye contact, deep and loving, seemed to last forever, and yet it couldn't have been more than an instant until he was kissing her again and moving even deeper within her, no more than an instant until they reached the height of their passion together with a force that seemed to take them racing through space at a speed far greater than the speed of the limousine.

Ella held on to him tightly while reality returned— the hum of the limo's motor, the feel of the seat against her back, the touch of Nick's flesh against hers. She took a deep steadying breath, opened her eyes slowly and smiled up at him. "Hi," she ventured almost shyly.

Nick grinned back and kissed her once more. "Hi, yourself." Laughing, he managed to pull her to an upright position, both of them struggling to rearrange their clothing and smooth back rumpled hair.

"Now *that* was a welcome..." Ella began.

Nick shook his head in amazement. "I confess I didn't plan it, but it's the story of my life with you." At her quizzical look, he went on. "As usual I start off calm, cool, collected, and within a very short time I'm very much out of control. A very undiplomatic approach, I'm afraid. Remember the reporters, Art, Yorba Linda?"

Ella snuggled close and rested her head against his chest. "All I remember is what happened a few minutes ago in this car." Then she sat up abruptly, eyes wide. From outside there came the unmistakable wail of a police siren. "Were we breaking some law?" Ella asked with a wicked smile.

Nick laughed. "That's just a precaution." He looked at her with a twinkle in his eyes. "In case we *do* break the law."

"Seriously, Nick—"

"Seriously, Ella," he countered, "a police escort just picked us up, and they'll be with us until we reach our destination."

"Which is?"

"Fox Haven."

Ella wasn't surprised, but she couldn't hide her concern, which she knew had always been evident to Nick. She didn't feel comfortable with the prospect of facing Mr. and Mrs. J. N. Manning.

He held her close and reassured her. "I'm taking you home to meet my parents. I should have done that a long time ago, but you put me off. You aren't putting me off any longer."

"This is unforgivably high-handed, Nick," she said, already forgiving him.

"As they say, if the mountain won't come to Mohammad..."

The sirens screamed louder as their limo slowed down momentarily and then shot forward.

"What's happening?" Ella asked.

"I have a feeling we're about to lose the phalanx of reporters who've been hot on our trail. The police stopped traffic behind us when we left the D.C. area and crossed into Virginia."

"Good planning," Ella said, admiring the effectiveness of her kidnapping.

"Thanks to my uncle the senator," Nick explained.

"Yes, of course," Ella responded. "The senator. But won't they have an inkling of where we're going?"

"Probably," Nick agreed, "but they won't follow."

"Thanks again to the efforts of your uncle the senator."

"Exactly," Nick said. "In desperation a man takes all the help he can get, Ella, and your man was desperate." He leaned over and kissed her thoroughly on the lips. "Desperate to see you, desperate to hold you, kiss you." Nick let his lips drift down her chin to the soft silkiness of her neck. "Wasn't it marvelous to return to our teenage years, making love in the back seat of a car? Very romantic," he said, hugging her closely. "Only you can make me a kid again, Ella."

"It was a first for me," she admitted.

He looked at her. "That's right. Cody saved you from the pangs of teenage romance. We'll have to do something about that. There's an old jukebox in the garage at Fox Haven. We can neck on the front porch swing."

"With your parents peeping through the curtains?"

"Of course. That only adds to the excitement." He gave her another hug. "This trip is for you, Ella, and I want you to enjoy every moment of it. I guarantee there'll be no interruptions. You don't even have to spend time with my parents if you don't want to."

"How do I avoid that?" she asked.

"We have a guest house. It's all yours. For resting, reading, watching TV, just taking it easy. I'll try not to press you about the future or even about the present. If you want me . . ."

He held her even closer, slipping his hand along her trim body, smoothing out her wrinkled skirt.

"I do want you," Ella said frankly, "and I do feel like the teenager I never really was."

"Then slip into my life, Ella, and see how it fits you. Someday—"

"You promised not to talk about the future," she warned.

"I promised to try," he corrected her. "But will you give my life-style a chance? It might look good on you."

At first Ella wasn't sure if she could even try the lifestyle on, let alone wear it well. Everything about it was alien to her, from the moment they drove up to the home, set miles off the main road among the rolling green hills of Virginia. It all bespoke great wealth but wealth far removed from the glitter of Hollywood. This was a well-being that was subtle, sedate and had been generations mellowing. It was a part of the rich soil, and as abiding as the roots of the spreading oak trees, as solid as the Georgian house, which was built of old brick turned a dusty pink with time. It made Ella feel insignificant, too new to the scene to even be counted.

Not that the Mannings didn't try to make her comfortable. If they were surprised to see their son arrive with Ella in tow, they were too well-mannered to let their feelings show. Welcoming her graciously, they showed her to the guest cottage to freshen up before joining them for dinner.

It was an uncomfortable meal for Ella even though she tried to relax and they tried to put her at ease. She blamed it all on the family portraits that lined the hall all the way to the dining room, where they were hung high on carved molding near the ceiling. Powdered wigs were neatly in place, uniforms resplendent, judges' robes appropriately dour. In every portrait the eyes seemed to be measuring and, Ella imagined, finding her wanting.

She was particularly disapproved of, Ella decided, by one of the more recent Manning men, probably Nick's grandfather, who looked very much like his handsome grandson. It was an aristocratic look, which, Ella suddenly realized, was just what set Nick apart from her. The look of his forebears, she was sure, would be the look of his descendants.

"They were really much nicer than they seem," Grace told Ella, putting her almost at ease with the rather mundane remark.

Ella managed to laugh as Nick agreed with his mother. "Not only were they for the most part unintimidating; some of them were downright likable, especially the scoundrels."

"Hush, Nick," his mother said. "Don't let any skeletons out of the closet."

It was an easy segue into talk of Ella and her family background, which she suspected Grace had put on the agenda earlier, but it couldn't have been very rewarding for her. Ella's knowledge of her background stopped with her grandparents, and even their history was sketchy.

Grace listened carefully to what little was offered and then moved graciously on to questions about Ella's present life and her volunteer work in Los Angeles. Ella sensed that there was an underlying need to know more, but propriety won out over curiosity and Grace refrained from asking the questions Ella felt certain were on the tip of her tongue, questions that would let the mother better understand the woman her son had brought to Fox Haven.

J.N., on the other hand, showed no particular curiosity. Ella guessed that he thought of her as the woman who could spoil his plans for his only son's career. He wasn't ready to embrace her either literally or figuratively she knew, but he wasn't rude or even cool to her. He welcomed her as Grace did, while his eyes, like those of his ancestors in the portraits, measured.

When the after-dinner conversation turned to politics, Grace suggested that the men take a walk in the garden while she and Ella had their coffee in the library.

"J.N. was dying to get outside for a cigarette," Grace told Ella when they were out of earshot, "and I like to give him the opportunity so he doesn't have to invent an excuse."

"You don't like him smoking?" Ella asked.

"He's not *supposed* to smoke because of his heart condition," Grace answered *sotto voce*, "but he has two or three a day. Of course, he knows I know, but both of us pretend. Anyway, political talk doesn't interest me in the least, and when he gets onto politics, I tend to change the subject. Then we go around in circles." Laughing jovially, Grace added, "I guess that makes life interesting at Fox Haven."

She settled down on the big flowered sofa. "Now, come on over and sit next to me and I'll show you the family photographs. I've finally gotten around to putting them all in albums, and I know you'll find them much more interesting than the portraits."

She was right. The photo albums gave them a chance to elaborate on a subject of mutual interest. Ella reflected that the fragile compatibility of her and Grace was based on their shared feelings for Nick, and there was certainly enough of Nick in the albums to supply an evening's conversation.

It started out well. Ella was charmed by the photographs, asking questions as Grace turned the pages of the album and delighting in the responses. But very soon Ella began to see a rigidity within the Manning family, which was all very evident in the pictures.

She'd always known how different her life-style was
from Nick's, but the difference had seemed vague and
general before. Now Ella was faced with documenta-
tion. The photographs, which showed Nick's life from
birth to adulthood, detailed his Manning heritage in a
very real way.

"He was always so bright," Grace told Ella. "That
was no surprise, of course, but his determination was
a bit more than we'd expected," she added with a
laugh. "Nick just never took *no* for an answer when
he felt he was right. Even as a little boy."

Ella looked at the childhood pictures as Grace
talked. They showed a fun-loving boy, engrossed in his
toys, his animals, his friends and family, but the look
was there, even on the babyish face. Nicholas Manning had always been a go-getter.

Ella smiled at the picture of him in his prep school
uniform, a little boy already adopting the stance of a
man, his course set.

"All the Mannings have gone to Deerfield Acad-
emy for well over two hundred years," Grace told her.
"I daresay if Nick had decided against it, there would
have been a battle royal, but Deerfield seemed to suit
him. It's in the blood, I suppose."

Grace continued to turn the pages, moving through
Nick's life and that of his sister, Julia, a dark-haired
girl who was the feminine counterpart of her brother.

"I especially like the Princeton photographs,"
Grace said as she reached the next stage in Nick's life,
his college years. "Maybe because Julia was a part of
them, too. You see, she married Nick's roommate,
Tom Carrington. Here they are at the winter ball. Nick
escorted Tom's sister. That never blossomed into a

romance, though," she said. A little sadly, Ella thought.

They passed through Princeton to Julia's wedding. "They're in Sweden now," Grace said, "where Tom's with the U.S. Trade Council. Here's their little boy, Tommy. He's enrolled in Deerfield already."

Ella smiled knowingly. No surprise there.

They were perusing the pages of J.N.'s sixty-fifth birthday when Nick and his father returned. As Grace pointed out the various guests, senators, congressmen, public servants and politicians, Ella realized that she wasn't boasting. They were all a part of Manning life and Nick's destiny.

"Mother, you're boring Ella to death," Nick said as he walked over to the sofa. He took the album from his mother and closed it forcefully. "Family albums are almost as bad as vacation slides."

"I wasn't bored at all," Ella said truthfully. "It was very enlightening."

Nick gave her a quizzical look before going to the bar to pour them a brandy nightcap. "Well, you've had enough for tonight, whether of boredom or enlightenment," he told Ella. "As soon as you finish that drink, I'm taking you to the guest house. It's been a long day."

No one objected to those instructions, least of all Ella. Without the albums as a buffer, she was fresh out of conversation and too tired to improvise.

Outside, the night was incredibly still, quiet except for the distant whinny of a horse. The lawn stretched for miles, it seemed to Ella, dark green in the moonlight, and the scent of the flowers bordering the walk signaled the beginning of spring.

"We've been in some beautiful settings together," Ella said. "This is certainly one of the best."

"Peaceful, too," Nick reminded her.

"It was peaceful in Yorba Linda," she answered. "For a while."

"This isn't California, Ella." They stopped beneath a live oak midway between the house and the guest cottage. Nick put his arm around her and buried his face in her hair. Somewhere a dog woke up, barked desultorily and settled back down to sleep. The horse whinnied again, and then all was silent.

"Listen to the peace," he told her. "This is Manning territory. You're safe here." He kissed her lightly on the neck.

"Watched over by a long line of Manning ancestors," she said.

"Is that so terrible?"

"No," Ella said. "It's rather comforting; just different, that's all. It's certainly not California."

"I'm sorry for what happened there, Ella. California is bad luck for us, I'm afraid."

"You don't need to be sorry," she told him. "Things just didn't work out."

"It'll be different here. This is where you belong, with my family, as a part of my family."

"Nick," she protested as they headed for the guest house, "I'm not even sure your parents like me."

"Of course they do."

"Only when we're talking about you."

"I've been away for years, and now I'm back. They have to steep themselves in me for a while. When everything returns to normal, you'll be surprised how quickly they take me for granted."

"Do you think everything will get back to normal? I mean the State Department, your career, all the ruckus over me?"

"Of course. It's already died down. After J.N. assures himself that my career is safe and Mom finds out that I have serious plans for my personal life, they'll welcome you with open arms. Right now they're just a little nonplussed by you," he said with a laugh. "After all, they weren't expecting their son to fall in love with Ella Butler. Wait a few days. That's all it'll take for them to feel completely comfortable with you."

Ella smiled up at him, trying not to wonder how long it would take *her* to feel comfortable.

Within a few days Ella had adjusted to life at Fox Haven, but she wondered if she could ever really adapt. Days progressed in an orderly, refined way at the estate. Much as always, Ella imagined. Manning generations might come and go but Fox Haven remained the same. There were some advantages, she had to admit: the newspapers seemed to have forgotten about them, and they were gloriously free from the pressures of the press.

She and Nick went into the small town just down the road on a shopping spree and bought riding clothes and boots, a sweater and long skirt for dinner, and a sexy black nightgown that Nick insisted on. Ella chose the skirt and sweater with care, keeping in her mind an image of Grace Manning and her understated but elegant taste. Then, after she'd paid for the clothes, Ella had gone back into the shop and bought a pair of long, dangling silver-filigree earrings. Grace compli-

mented her on the outfit that night at dinner but stu-
diously avoided mentioning the earrings.

Within a few days, Ella was learning to ride horseback with an English saddle, giving Grace pointers on
gardening that she'd picked up over the years from
Joe, and even singing duets after dinner with J.N., but
she still felt very much a guest, not a part of the family.

The nights were for Nick, and they were perfect.
Then a phone call came from the State Department
telling Nick that the first of his fact-finding missions
had been set up.

The day Ella and Nick were to leave, Ella woke up
slowly, stretched and remembered what had happened in the night. It was so wonderful to sleep with
him again, she thought, so perfect. There was only one
world when they were together, and it belonged to
them alone. When he reached out for her and she
welcomed him, that was their reality. When he slipped
inside of her, it was always as if he were coming home
where he belonged. And when they lay side by side
after making love, her body curled against his, Nick's
leg anchoring hers, she felt safe.

"This is the way it should be," he'd told her so
often, and in her heart, Ella knew that he was right.
Yet the outside always intruded. It was intruding again
today. In a matter of hours, she would be on a plane
back to Los Angeles and Nick would be at the State
Department, preparing for his fact-finding mission.
While Nick was overseas, Ella would begin her new
life. He'd be gone at least a month, time for her to find
another place to live and try it on her own, time to give

a signal to Cody's fans that she was no longer their property.

Most important, there would be time to find out what kind of life Ella really did fit into. She still believed it was at neither La Casa nor Fox Haven but somewhere in between. The discovery of just where might not please Nick; that much she knew, but she had to please herself to be a whole person and not become an appendage of the Mannings as she'd once been of Cody.

"Good morning, sleepyhead." Nick stood in the bedroom doorway, holding a coffee tray. "I think I've finally mastered the espresso machine. Wait until you taste this." Nick brought the tray to the bedside and put it on the table. Ella started to get up, but he put out a hand to restrain her. "No, stay there. We're spending this morning in bed. No jogs, no horseback, no luncheon with my parents, just lolling together in the feathers," he said with a wicked smile. "Now taste."

Ella took a sip of the coffee he offered. "Hmm. Nearly perfect."

"Nearly?" He took the cup from her and tasted. "It *is* perfect." Balancing it carefully, he climbed into bed beside Ella. "What could compare with my life at the moment? The perfect woman and the perfect cup of coffee."

"The perfect cigar?" she offered.

"Except I don't smoke. I do, however, drink coffee and..." He let the thought linger as they shared the coffee lovingly between kisses. Then he put the cup away and took her in his arms.

"I've missed you," he said, brushing her hair back off her forehead. "I never know how much until I touch you again."

"It's only been about ten minutes," Ella reminded him.

"Hmm," he said as his hand strayed across her shoulder and drifted to the soft roundness of her breast. "I have a short memory, and I have to refresh it frequently." He rubbed his palm across her nipple and under his touch it tautened for him. "Oh, yes," he said huskily. "Now I remember." And he knew, as Ella knew, that the heat that had built so quickly between them couldn't be quelled until they'd made love again, slowly, lazily and completely.

When at last they were satiated, wrapped together, their bodies damp but cooled, Nick spoke to her softly again. "I love you," he said.

"I love you, too," Ella told him, burying her head in the crook of his arms, safe and protected. That's what he wanted to give her, love and protection, and that's what she always found with him.

"Listen," he said softly.

Ella cocked her head. "I can't hear anything."

"Exactly," Nick replied. "No Cody Butler fans singing, no Art Newcombe bursting in, no photographers or reporters."

"It is peaceful," Ella agreed.

"It's a good life, in spite of all the traditions that you object to."

"I don't object. I just find it all very overpowering. This compound, Deerfield, Princeton, careers in public service. Being a Manning entails a great deal of responsibility."

"And rewards," he reminded her. "You'd be a great Manning."

"Are you proposing?" she teased him.

"I am, and I'll continue to do so. I want to take care of you, to make your life the best it can be. I want to protect you, Ella."

She turned in his arms and looked up at him. "I love you, Nick. There's no one else in my life or my heart, but I need to do the things *I* need to do, without being protected."

"We've had this talk before," he admitted, "and it always ends the same way. You want to be in charge of your life—your new life."

"I will be," she said determinedly. "I hope you believe that, Nick."

"I think I'm beginning to."

"Good, because I've started looking for a place of my own; at least Nikki has started looking. I have to stay out of the way. As soon as realtors hear Cody Butler's widow wants a house, the prices escalate. But I'll find something soon, and it'll be mine. All mine."

"And I just have to let you get out there on your own, unprotected?"

"Yes," she said stubbornly. "You urged me to leave La Casa, remember?"

"That's true. I wanted you away from the Cody mystique but not alone."

"I've been protected long enough behind La Casa's walls. I *have* to do this alone."

"All right," he said. "I'll be gone a month, six weeks at the most. I'll give you that long to get established and make your point."

"Don't be condescending, Nick. I'm serious about this."

"Oh, I realize you are, Ella, but so am I. As soon as I get back from this mission, we're going to have the talk we've been putting off. This living on opposite coasts is impossible."

"If you get an ambassadorship—"

"It would be overseas, but I'd have a base, a home you could share with me."

"Behind the walls of an embassy residence," Ella said, more to herself than to Nick, "protected."

Chapter 10

I almost wish I hadn't seen him in Virginia," Ella told Nikki.

"What are you saying?"

Ella laughed. "It's true. Being with him so long, so intimately, there at the cottage just makes being without him that much more painful." This was true; Ella could hardly sleep at night thinking about being nestled in Nick's arms with his breath against her cheek, sweet and loving. That's not all that interrupted her sleep, however. Her thoughts were often very erotic and her dreams, when she did manage to sleep, even more so. She relived their lovemaking in the limousine over and over. The night before when they'd talked on the phone, she'd confessed that.

"I told him how much I missed him," she said to Nikki. "I told him in graphic detail, in fact."

"Ella, how brazen," Nikki said with a giggle. "What did he say?"

"The connection was terrible. He's somewhere in Africa, and I don't think he heard me, but when he calls today, I'm going to repeat every word."

Nikki giggled again just as the phone rang. When she answered, Ella thought she saw a blush rise to her friend's cheeks.

"It's Nick," Nikki said. "I'm getting out of here. All that sexy talk would be too much for me." Picking up her coffee cup from the desk, Nikki headed for the kitchen. Ella was already deep in conversation when the door closed behind her.

"Today's call was even less satisfying than before," Ella said as she got into Nikki's car outside La Casa. "This time I couldn't hear *him*, and he's not going to be calling again for a week."

"Why?" Nikki started the car and pulled out of the circular driveway.

"He's going to be in remote, almost inaccessible areas, some of them with no phone service of any kind, good or bad."

"Duck!" Nikki warned as the guard opened the gates and she drove through, hitting the accelerator of her sports car. "Okay, we're safe," she told Ella a few moments later.

"How were the crowds?" Ella asked, looking back over her shoulder toward the house.

"Only a handful of kids, and I'm pretty sure they didn't see you. We'll know in a minute." At the next corner, she turned sharply, pulled up to the curb and waited. A chauffeured Mercedes passed with an elderly woman in the back. "I would venture to say they're not hot on our trail," Nikki commented. "Whoops, this one doesn't look good," she added as a beat-up station wagon approached, rock music blaring from the speakers.

"It's okay," Ella told her, based on her long experience studying pursuers. "There are surfboards on top of the car. Just kids going to the beach."

Cautiously, Nikki pulled out into the street and glanced again over her shoulder. "All clear. We're on the way to Malibu. Wait until you see this house. It's a buyer's dream, as our realtor says."

It was everything Nikki had maintained, a beautiful beach house with rustic charm but all the modern conveniences. "Jacuzzi, heated pool, sprinkler system, burglar alarm," Nikki listed as they walked through the house. "Best of all is the look of the place, Ella. It's you."

Ella didn't answer right away. Instead, she walked out onto the porch with Nikki following. The house overlooked a long stretch of sand that was nearly deserted in late afternoon. The sea gulls soared all around, claiming the beach for themselves. "My life seems to move me from one beautiful location to another," she mused.

"You're complaining?" Nikki came up and stood next to Ella at the porch railing.

"Not complaining, just commenting. I don't really feel like I belong in any of the settings I'm thrust into."

"Then what are you looking for, Ella?"

"I don't know. There doesn't seem to be a place for me."

"Well, maybe this house isn't right, but we'll find one that is. Just you wait."

"I'm not talking about that, Nikki. It's not this house or another house. It's more a lack of direction. If I knew what I wanted, I would know where I was going." Ella smiled. "That certainly sounds vague enough, but I know what I mean." Laughing outright, she added, "I think."

"I thought you wanted Nick."

"Yes, I do."

"Then your place is wherever he goes."

"That's exactly what he says. But wherever Nick goes, his roots are at Fox Haven, and I just don't seem to fit in there. Lord," she said, shaking off the feeling of despair that was beginning to overcome her. "If I don't watch out, I'm going to get maudlin. You had another house to look at, didn't you, Nikki?"

"Two more."

"Good. Let's go see them. I don't think Malibu is for me."

"Well, you have to stay in the vicinity," Nikki argued, "because you're spending almost all of your time at the hospital."

Nikki was right about that. During the two weeks since she'd returned to Los Angeles, Ella had given almost full-time attention to plans for the clinic on Kikao, working on the telephone in Susan Dunne's office.

She was there again the next day, having left Nikki to search out more real estate possibilities on her own. "I believe this takes care of the last government permit," Ella said as she put down the phone and glanced up at Susan. "I've talked to the powers that be twice a day, every day, and it finally paid off."

"Great." Susan poured herself a cup of coffee. "That means Doug and I can leave next week as planned."

"I don't see why not," Ella agreed. "The large downstairs room should be ready by then. Our Kikao foreman is doing a great job, and the rest of the remodeling of the villa can go on while you're beginning to see patients. It'll just be a little noisy, that's all."

"I'm certainly not going to complain," Susan said. "Just so we're *there*."

"Everything's moving so fast," Ella said. "Your replacements here at the hospital are ready to take over. The clinic's ready to open—"

"Thanks to you," Doug said, appearing as he often did just in time to comment on the conversation between Ella and his wife. "But I wouldn't mind delaying things for another week or so...."

"Don't say that, Doug," Susan objected. "I'm almost packed."

"I'm not about to rush this at the expense of Ella's health."

Ella looked up questioningly.

"You've been glued to that phone for almost twelve hours a day, and the strain is beginning to show," Doug told her.

"I am a little tired," Ella admitted.

Susan raised her eyebrows in surprise. "That's a first, Ella Butler admitting that she's not feeling absolutely perfect."

"I think maybe the hospital food is getting to me," Ella ventured. "Too many hamburgers and fries from the cafeteria don't make for a balanced diet. My stomach has been a little queasy," she added.

"Then one of my last acts will be to give you a thorough checkup," Susan announced.

"I can't today, Susan. There's too much to do—"

"Today," Susan demanded. "It'll take no more than half an hour to run some tests and do a little blood work."

Ella, adamant, was shaking her head. "I promise to leave early tonight, eat a good dinner and go straight to bed, but for now I need to talk to you about the last shipment from Balboa over to Kikao. I have a loading order—"

Ella felt the pressure of Doug's hand on her shoulder. "Susan's right, Ella. The sooner you get checked out, the better."

"Doug, I don't have time—"

"Ella," they cautioned her, both speaking at the same time.

"All right," she agreed with a sigh, standing up to hug each of them. "I don't know what I'll do without the two of you when you go to Kikao."

"Come over there for your checkups," Doug suggested.

"I'm being serious, Doug. I'll really miss you."

Doug hugged her mightily. "That goes for us, too, but there's no reason why you can't come along."

"Don't tempt me," Ella said as she followed Susan into the examining room. "I'd love to be there for the opening of the clinic."

* * *

Ella sent the limousine away. She'd decided to walk for a while, and since almost no one ever walked in Los Angeles except when shopping, she didn't expect to attract any crowds. The hospital wasn't located in the most fashionable section of the city in any case; in fact, Cal had warned her that it might even be unsafe when she tried to send him on his way.

"I'd better follow you, Mrs. Butler," he suggested.

"No. My walking with you following along will really create a commotion," Ella said. "I'll tell you what. I'm going to walk to the corner of Wilshire and Highland, but I'm going to take my time. I may even stop along the way. Meet me there in an hour."

Cal, still unsure, finally agreed to let her go, but Ella had the feeling he would be within shouting distance, just in case she had to shout. Well, she felt like shouting, Ella thought, but she would refrain. Besides, she didn't know whether to shout for joy or out of wonder or from sheer amazement. All she knew was that the past hour had changed her life.

Nothing would be the same again, and she certainly wasn't going to face her feelings by getting into a limo and going back to La Casa. That was not the place to think about herself and Nick—and their baby.

When Susan had told her what she suspected and what she subsequently verified, Ella had sat on the examining table, staring off into space in a daze.

"You should at least get that strange expression off your face," Susan had told her. "You look a little loony."

"That's exactly how I feel."

"Didn't you have any idea?"

"Not the slightest. I've always been something of a medical puzzle when it came to my cycle; I was told that it would be very difficult for me to ever get pregnant."

Susan laughed. "Well, you were told wrong; you are very definitely and healthily pregnant."

That conversation had been less than an hour ago. Only now was she beginning to face the fact that she was pregnant. The love she'd shared with Nick had produced life, the baby growing inside her. Ella was happy, and she knew Nick would share her happiness. Of course, she would tell him, but it would be almost a week before he called again so she had time. Time to think.

As Ella walked along the palm-tree-bordered street, she thought of herself as an alien in Los Angeles. This wasn't her home any more than Texas was her home. Or Virginia.

Yet in a way her unborn child already had a home, and that was Fox Haven. Nick would want a house in the compound. He and his family would expect the baby to go to Deerfield and then Princeton, later become a judge or a senator and lead a very privileged life. What if her baby wanted another kind of life?

Ella thought about her conversation with Grace Manning. Nick had been a strong-willed boy, his mother had admitted, and if he'd rebelled against family tradition, there would have been what Grace called a "battle royal." He didn't rebel; the life that had been planned for him suited him. He thrived on it; it gave him sustenance.

And what if that life didn't fit the new addition to the Manning family? There was another strain in the bloodline now. Ella Butler was the unknown quantity, for her roots weren't sunk deeply in any soil, and what she would pass on to her child was as yet undetermined.

Ella stopped at a little restaurant with tables set up outside that were empty but tempting in the midafternoon. She put on her dark glasses and took her place at one of them. The waiter recognized her but was polite enough not to acknowledge the fact as he took her order of a salad and a diet drink. It was time to change her eating habits.

Ella saw Cal, waiting and watching a block away, at the wheel of the limo. She was being protected as she'd always been and as Nick assured she would be in their life together, she and now the baby. That should have given her a good feeling, but it didn't. Instead, the feeling she had was one of foreboding. She'd asked Nick for time, time to take hold of her life before being swept up in his. Now her time was running out. As soon as Nick found out about the baby, he would be in control and all her choices would be taken away. There was one way to extend her time, which hit Ella just as the waiter placed the salad in front of her. She almost cried out. She had the perfect solution to her problem.

"You're what? No, don't answer," Nikki said as she paced around Ella's office.

"I've already answered, Nikki."

"I must have heard you wrong."

Ella laughed. "Then I'll tell you again. I'm not buying a house at Malibu or anywhere else. I'm moving to Kikao."

"You don't mean just visiting; you mean moving?"

"Exactly," Ella said. Her laughter was joyful. She felt wonderfully free now that her decision was made. "I may stay a few months, or maybe I'll stay a few years. Who knows?"

Nikki finally settled in a wicker chair opposite Ella, who'd been sitting calmly throughout the conversation. "When you break out, you really break out, don't you?"

"Let's just say I'm a slow starter, but I pick up speed."

Nikki stared at Ella for a long time. "You really are serious." It was a statement, a foregone conclusion.

"Perfectly."

"When are you leaving?"

"As soon as I can get everything taken care of here. I hope to be ready in time to go with the Dunnes. Less than a week," she said. "Oh, Nikki, it's going to be wonderful. You know how my heart and soul is in the clinic. I'll miss the children here terribly, but they don't need me nearly as much."

"You've certainly worked hard enough to pull it all together, not just financing the clinic but organizing the whole thing, coordinating between here and the islands. It was a tremendous effort, and you pulled it off. I hope they name the clinic after you and not Cody."

Ella smiled. "The name doesn't matter. I feel good about it, and it's going to take care of a great need. I want to continue to be a part of the clinic."

"Then go for it, Ella." Nikki paused with a frown. "What about Nick? Have you told him you're leaving?"

"No. He's somewhere in Africa, remember? I'll be gone before he calls again."

"He'll certainly be surprised when I tell him—"

"You're not going to tell him, Nikki."

"What?" Nikki leaned forward in her chair, clearly puzzled again.

"I don't want Nick to know where I am, and I'll need your help."

"Oh, no." Nikki was adamant. "I'm not going to aid and abet you in avoiding Nick Manning."

"Just for a while, Nikki."

Nikki was fervently shaking her head. "Nope. He's the best thing that's ever happened to you, and I'm not going to be a party to your breakup."

"This isn't a breakup, Nikki. There's too much holding us together," Ella said as she touched her abdomen surreptitiously. "I just need a little time."

"You want him, don't you?"

"Yes," Ella admitted, "but not just on his terms. So much has happened that I've reached the point where I can't process it all." Ella didn't need to tell Nikki the latest development to make that statement believable; a great deal *had* happened between her and Nick in the few brief months since they had met: the love affair, the meetings in hideaways across the country, the arguments, the tension. Now, most important of all, their baby. She wouldn't tell Nikki yet, knowing her friend would never be able to keep the news from Nick. And it had to be kept from him, at least for now.

"Give me time, Nikki, to pull everything together."

"You promise it's not over?"

"I promise."

"Well, if you promise, then I'll promise, but that doesn't mean I agree."

They both laughed. "We sound like a couple of Girl Scouts," Ella said.

"Just so our Girl Scout pledge includes eventual reunion with Nick," Nikki insisted one final time. "What about this?" she asked, spreading her arms to include all of La Casa.

"That's the other thing I need to talk to you about. Do you think you could stay on, Nikki?"

"Sure. I like having the extra money and, I might add, so does Frank. A professor's income needs supplementing. But what would I do?"

"You'd be coordinator of the Cody Butler Estate."

"What in the world does that mean?"

Ella explained. "It means that La Casa is going to be open to the public."

"I don't believe it. You said you'd never—"

"Never say never, I guess." Ella had been busy in the twenty-four hours since Susan had broken the news to her about the baby. For once in her life, she had a clear path to follow, and she was walking it resolutely. "The packers are going to put all my belongings into storage, and by the end of the month La Casa will be ready to open. Art's taking care of the press releases. You'll be coordinating everything with him."

"Hmm," Nikki mouthed tentatively.

"You can handle Art, Nikki."

"True," Nikki admitted, "but how will *he* handle all this? It's the end of an era, really."

"It's only the end of my part; the rest will stay the same, and that's all Art cares about. Cody's memory will live on," Ella said. "In a way, I imagine Art's glad to get rid of me. I've caused too many problems lately."

"Does he know where you're going?"

"No, and he's not to know. I've told him I'm having health problems and need to get away. Actually, he was so tickled over getting his hands on Cody's house, he hardly paid attention. But he'll do a good job—with you riding shotgun. Just don't let him bring in neon signs or sell popcorn in the dining room."

"Or auction off the china," Nikki added.

Ella giggled. "I don't care if he does, but Art won't. Everything in La Casa is sacred to him. I can depend on him, and on you."

"The legend will go on, but you won't be a part of it. You really surprised me this time, Ella."

"Guess what. I really surprised myself. If Nick had been here, everything would be different. He would have kept me from going to Kikao, and I would have been glad. It all has to do with timing. He's not here; he can't keep me from going, and I'm still glad. I have a niche somewhere, Nikki. It's not here, and it's certainly not at Malibu. Maybe I'll find it on Kikao."

More than two weeks passed before Nick got a chance to call Ella again. The answering service picked up, and the connection was bad. He called again the next day after an almost sleepless night of wondering where she was and how she was, expecting to hear her voice on the other end of the line. It was seven o'clock in the morning in California. She wouldn't have left for the hospital that early. Yet she didn't answer, and neither did Juanita. That was what worried Nick. No one answered. Finally, the service picked up again. The operator was noncommittal. She could only take a message. She didn't know the whereabouts of Mrs. Butler or her staff.

Nick managed to get through the day, meeting with the *chargés d'affaires* at the embassy, reviewing plans for the next post he would visit, but the whole time his mind was on Ella. He'd waited a week to hear her voice, and his disappointment was keen.

There were still two more posts to visit before returning to Washington. Once there he could get a handle on what was going on, but until then all he could do was call and reach the answering service. Finally his frustration began to get the best of him and set his imagination working. He saw her going out with other men, ignoring the press or even hiding from them as she'd done with him.

Nick had been used to getting his own way all his life. It came naturally to him, and although he never would have considered giving orders to women, they tended to do as he wished. Until Ella had come along. She was the woman he wanted, the only one he'd ever really wanted. Something—he had never really known what—was keeping her from him. She'd said she needed time, and he'd finally relented and agreed to give it to her, but he planned for that to end when he got home. Press or no press, he was going to go after her and marry her.

* * *

"What do you mean disconnected?" Nick shouted into the telephone.

"The private number you asked me to try has been disconnected, Mr. Manning," Gavin Reid's secretary answered calmly. "Is there another you'd like to try?"

"Yes," Nick said. "Get a man named Art Newcombe in Hollywood. I don't have the number, but I'm sure he's listed. He's Cody Butler's manager."

"Cody Butler's been dead for years, Mr. Manning."

"I know. Strange, isn't it, but he still has a manager," Nick said, hanging up the phone and waiting for a response from Gavin. When none came, he said, "Sorry, Gavin, but I've been gone almost two months, and for the last half of that time, I haven't been able to talk with her. Damn it, it was bad enough when I got no answer; now the number has been disconnected."

"Maybe it would be a good idea to let it drop, Nick."

"Is that a threat, Gav?"

Gavin frowned deeply. "Of course not, my friend. Only a suggestion. This relationship is taking its toll on you."

"On the contrary, Gavin," Nick said, his dark eyes narrowing. "I've done some of my best work for State in the past six weeks."

"I didn't mean—"

"And my future here, however it's presently defined, will be based on the quality of my work and nothing else, I sincerely hope."

Before Gavin had a chance to respond, Nick had
turned and walked out of the office, pausing at the
secretary's desk long enough to hear that Art Newcombe was not in and a message had been left for him
to return Nick's call.

"Fat chance of that," Nick replied irreverently to
the news, remembering to thank the young woman
politely so she would know it was not she but her boss
who was the subject of Nick's wrath, not she but Art
Newcombe who was the subject of his scorn.

But all that wrath and all that scorn benefited Nick
little. Another day passed, and he was no closer to
finding Ella. He couldn't remember Nikki's last name,
probably had never known it. He didn't even know the
name of the hospital where Ella did so much volunteer work. He was realizing finally, much too late, how
little he knew about the woman he professed to love.
He'd been so wrapped up in her that he'd really never
seen her.

It had been a selfish love affair, based on what *he*
wanted. All that time she'd been trying to find herself, and he hadn't even understood. Now she was on
her own, without him, and finally he realized how serious she'd been. It was time for her needs, and if he
found her, when he found her, he wouldn't forget that
again.

It was no surprise that Art Newcombe never returned the call. Nick didn't even try to reach him
again. This wasn't the time to depend on others. First
thing the next morning, without even bothering to
pack a bag, he headed for the airport. He'd pick up
anything he needed when he got there. Whatever happened to Ella, she'd been in Los Angeles the last time

he'd talked to her, and that's where he was going to begin his search.

He'd bought a ticket and was walking toward his terminal when the headlines of a tabloid caught his eye. He stopped in his tracks, staring at it through the glass doors of the newsstand. Then he went inside, bought the paper and opened it to the story.

Ella pushed up the sleeves of her cotton dress, poured herself a glass of juice and walked to the doorway of the villa to look outside. It was a mild, clear day, and the hills of Kikao looked turquoise against the pale blue sky. Far in the distance to the west she could see the ocean, which was another shade of blue, almost aqua. Ella breathed deeply, infused in the colors of this perfect day. But something marred it, and that something was in the corner of Ella's mind, lodged deeply.

"It's paradise," Susan said as she approached and stood beside Ella.

"*Almost* paradise," Ella corrected her.

"You're still worried about the photographer, aren't you?"

Ella nodded. "I don't think he bought our cover-up story."

Susan couldn't help laughing. "Well, I thought it was pretty good for a spur-of-the-moment invention. It's not so farfetched to think you could be Doug's sister. Your coloring is similar."

"And he's only about twice as big," Ella said with a laugh.

"And half as neat."

Ella laughed. "Those things can be explained away. What probably did me in was my entrance into the clinic doing fifty miles an hour, and my appearance. Lord, I could have put on a muumuu or something, but no, I burst in wearing shorts and looking five months pregnant."

"You *are* five months pregnant, Ella," Susan reminded her.

"But it's not even noticeable in a dress. The dumb part is, I knew he was here doing the story. I was just so excited about the little Balu boy's recovery that I rushed in to see him and almost knocked down the photographer."

"Well, it's over now, and there's nothing we can do. Except maybe wonder why Doug didn't wrestle him to the ground and take his camera away."

They both laughed at the idea of Doug acting aggressively.

Ella finished her juice as she watched kids playing out in front of the villa. "You're right. It's all over, and all he has is a picture of a plump woman in shorts who may or may not be Doug's sister."

"Not what you'd call a description of Ella Butler," Susan said.

"Not yesterday's Ella Butler, in any case," Ella commented.

"Besides, isn't Nikki dropping hints in the gossip columns that you are off at a spa in Mexico?"

"Those were her instructions, to plant a story that I'm shedding a few pounds." Ella laughed as she folded her arms across what was becoming an ample belly. "I'm sure she did her job well, but in that world everything is suspect, and I can't help worrying that some enterprising newsman will track me down, though Lord knows I was sneaky enough getting out of L.A."

"You're really concerned that Nick will find out, aren't you?"

"He will find out," Ella answered, "but I just didn't want him to read about it in the newspaper."

"Then why don't you call him?" Susan inquired.

"Not yet. I need a little more time."

"Well, you know what they say: You can run, but you can't hide."

The kids playing in the yard had gotten into a brawl, and Susan went out to separate them before they did further damage to injuries that had just been treated. Ella watched for a few minutes and then turned to go back into the villa.

Each time she walked down the hall past rooms that had been set up for examining and treating patients, Ella couldn't suppress her joy. It had all worked! The villa was a functioning clinic even though there was still a long way to go. The X-ray facilities weren't yet complete; the lab was set up, but a top-notch technician was proving difficult to find; only two rooms had been converted to overnight hospital care, and there was a long line of patients ready to be admitted.

Still, the progress was phenomenal, and they'd done it all against great odds. Logistically, it hadn't seemed possible, but the islanders had proved they could transport equipment, haul it to the site and set it up without a hitch. They wanted this clinic even more than the Dunnes and Ella did; they were determined, and their determination had made things work.

Ella went into her first-floor office, which had once been a storage room. She'd decorated it with pictures of the island, but there were still boxes stacked in all the corners. She'd get to them eventually. First things first. And today there was a long list to supersede the boxes: four mothers were due for instruction in prenatal care in addition to the TB tests and immunizations scheduled, and of course there would be the walk-in patients. That group was enlarging daily. As the news spread from island to island about the new clinic, boats began to arrive with adults and children needing treatment.

The clinic was able to help them all; it was working, and Ella couldn't have been more thrilled. Yet nothing could quite cover up the need that was burning deep inside of her, a need for Nick. Even the exhaustion after her long working hours didn't bring sleep at the end of the day. As tired as she was when she fell into bed, Ella still lay awake in her room on the second story of the villa, thinking of Nick. The time had come to tell him about their baby.

Chapter 11

Ella was on the overseas phone lines early the next morning, ready to talk to Nick. She'd missed him desperately; more than that, she was ready to tell him about his child. It was unfair of her to wait any longer. After the inevitable delays, replete with fractured connections and a strange singing in the lines, Ella finally got through and met disappointment. No one knew where he was. She reached Gavin Reid's office in Washington only to find out that Gavin was in New York for the day and the secretary had no idea how to reach Nick.

"He was here a couple of days ago, Mrs. Butler, trying to get hold of *you*, but I don't know where he is now. You might try him in Virginia."

His parents were no more helpful. According to Nick's mother, he'd been there for a day or two when he'd returned from his trip and they hadn't seen him since.

Ella finally reached Gavin in New York, but Nick's boss was equally vague.

"I can't help you at all, Mrs. Butler. He left my office in a somewhat turbulent mood. I had the idea he might be going to California."

Ella's next call was to Nikki, whom she finally tracked down at her sons' school in the mountains.

"You told me not to let Nick know anything, Ella," Nikki reminded her.

"I've changed my mind," Ella said.

"Well, he hasn't called me, but he's reached the service several times. I told them to play dumb."

"Well, change the instructions, Nikki. I'm ready to talk to him now, so tell the service to give him the number here at the clinic."

With that, Ella settled back to wait, expecting to hear from him before the morning was over. Nick was persistent. He would call the service again; of that she was sure.

Her wait was made more bearable by the activity at the clinic that morning. Ella spent the first hour training the new receptionist and setting up appointments for the next day. By ten o'clock there was a whirlwind of activity in the clinic, and she forgot all about phone calls.

A little boy had been brought in on a makeshift stretcher from one of the smallest and most distant islands in the chain. He was three years old but looked no more than ten or twelve months. Much too weak to walk, he was so thin it broke Ella's heart just to look at him. She stood by as Doug examined and tested the boy and later heard the diagnosis with despair.

"It's hopeless, Ella," Doug told her.

"Why?" she cried.

"He has a rare congenital heart disease that's incurable without surgery. Even with the operation, there's less than a fifty-fifty chance of survival."

"Fifty-fifty is good enough for me," Ella declared. The child, with his huge black eyes looking to her for comfort, completely won Ella's heart.

"We have to be realistic," Doug said as he led Ella down the hall to her office. "There's no way we can perform the surgery this boy needs. This is a *clinic*, Ella. We can handle some cardiology problems, but not this kind of surgery. There are only a dozen or so hospitals in the United States equipped for—"

"Is there one in Los Angeles?"

Doug nodded.

"Then we'll send him there," Ella declared.

"It's a long trip," he answered thoughtfully.

"So was the boat trip from his island," Ella argued, "not to mention the jeep trip into the hills."

"That's true," Doug admitted.

"Could he survive it?"

"Yes," Doug said, "if careful preparations were made."

"Leave that to me," Ella said determinedly.

It was late afternoon before Ella had made all the arrangements and was able to relax over a cup of coffee in the office.

"I don't believe it," Susan said, coming in to join her. "You have surgery set up for him at the best facility in L.A. on Tuesday morning?"

"Yep," Ella replied. "And with one of the country's top surgeons. The boy's leaving tomorrow."

Susan shook her head in wonder. "Sometimes I think you're more than one person, Ella. Doug said he also pulled you in to help set that fracture this morning while I was busy in prenatal care."

"Even with the new doctor assisting, I was a little nervous," Ella said. "Fortunately, the nurse I hired will be here in less than a week."

"Fortunate indeed," Susan said, "because you're working too hard at too many jobs. In fact, as your physician, I'm going to prescribe the afternoon off—what's left of it." It was already four o'clock.

Ella was happy to comply. Late afternoon was her favorite time on the island, and she looked forward to a long walk before twilight. Since she and the Dunnes arrived on Kikao, Ella had become friends with many of the islanders, and she enjoyed taking part in their afternoon kava ceremony.

Ella joined the men sitting cross-legged on the ground to drink kava from a coconut shell. Although their women didn't participate, they'd decided Ella was different and welcomed her into the circle. The first time Ella had tried to keep up with the men she had realized very quickly that the drink, extracted from the roots of kava plants, was not only flavorful but also alcoholic. For the baby's sake she'd learned to take only a sip of the liquid while observing the ceremony politely.

After it was over, she continued her walk down through the hills until she reached the outskirts of the seaside village where she and Nick had been strolling so casually the day their boat had left them stranded.

She smiled in remembrance. Her thoughts of him were strong and vital, but after her long day at the clinic, Ella felt wary again about what would happen when she finally talked with Nick. She was almost glad she hadn't reached him. Even though the inevitable was only being put off, she was gaining time to analyze her feelings.

"It's possible to overanalyze," Susan had told her. "Sometimes these things just have to be played by ear. Until you hear his reaction, there's no way to predict."

"I know what his reaction will be," Ella had answered with certainty. "He'll want me to leave here, Susan."

Ella still wasn't sure she could do that. Except for those long hours in the middle of the night when she yearned for him, she was happy, reluctant to think about leaving the clinic where she'd found herself, her home. There was no way Nick would agree with that assessment of her future and her worth. He'd want her to be with him, wherever he went. No longer *Cody's widow*, she would become the *Ambassador's wife*.

That's not what she wanted for herself, not now when she was watching her dream come true at the clinic. She'd survive the nights; they would get easier.

Physically, Ella had never felt so good in her life. She knew that she looked as good as she felt. The hard work she performed daily and her long walks had kept her from gaining too much weight. The sun had brightened her cheeks, and as Doug had mentioned often, there was a light in her eyes that hadn't been there before. That light came from her baby, Nick's baby.

Ella walked back to the top of the hill slowly and then stopped to look down on the beach far in the distance. It could have been there beside the beach at Kikao that their baby had begun its life. She liked to think that their child had been conceived on that wonderful night she and Nick spent in that little hut by the sea. She couldn't see the hut from here. It was nestled in the palm trees out of sight. But her memory of that night was beautifully vivid, and she had a strong desire for the baby to be born here, where everything had begun.

Walking along the edge of the cliff, Ella smiled to herself when she thought about all that had happened since Nikki had jokingly suggested that she consider "making a baby." Ella had thrown a pillow at her friend and determined that she could never be so calculating. Well, she'd been right about that. There was nothing calculating about what had happened between her and Nick. The baby just beginning to kick inside of her was a product of love.

In such a short time, she had found everything she wanted, a man to love, a baby on the way, a place where she was needed and where she was happy.

There was one problem. While she had all the pieces of her life, they didn't fit together. Nick was separated from her and the baby, far away from Kikao.

Ella finished her walk a little sadly, greeting some of the island men who were busy working on their outrigger canoe. Their lean brown bodies glistened in the late-afternoon sun; their handsome faces glowed with good humor. Ella was one of them, and that made her happy and proud. This *was* her home.

* * *

But there was that lonely stretch in the early morning when she woke again, tossing in her bed at the clinic and wanting Nick fiercely. She tried to put it out of her mind when dawn came; she got up and dressed in the pale light. She tried to look ahead to the busy day when she'd get the little boy, whose name was Tonka, ready for his trip to America.

Tonka was a bright child, and he understood what was happening. He was going to get well so he could play like the other boys. Ella accompanied him on the boat trip to Balboa and sat beside him in the car as they drove to the airport, talking about the adventure that lay ahead. His smile reminded her of little Donnie at the Children's Hospital. Someday, she hoped, Tonka would be just as happy and active.

The medical plane was ready for them when they reached the airport. Tonka's older sister, an unusually mature and serious girl, was traveling with him. They would be met in Los Angeles and taken straight to the hospital. The medics on the plane were well prepared for any problem, and Ella waved them off with a good feeling. Tonka would make it.

"When will we know?" she asked Doug when she returned to the clinic.

"The first twenty-four hours after the surgery are critical," he told her. "If he makes it through that—"

"When—not if," Ella corrected him.

Doug smiled understandingly. "The recovery should take about six weeks, and he'll be home in less than two months," Doug said positively.

"Before my baby's born," Ella said.

"Yes. He'll be here in time to greet the new arrival. So you are planning to stay on, Ella?"

"Yes," Ella said firmly. "I can't imagine any place I belong more."

Before the day ended, she had reason to wonder whether that was true or not.

Ella was alone in the examining room, straightening up for the patients who would be seen the next day. She was humming softly to herself as she pulled down a clean paper sheet to cover the table. The tune was an old Southern cradle song she'd learned in Texas many years before.

"That sounds like a lullaby," a voice said.

Ella turned around, startled. Nick stood in the doorway, and there were two things she noticed about him immediately. The first was how handsome he looked even though his hair seemed grayer at the temples and he'd lost a little weight. Then she noticed the anger in his eyes.

Nick had tried to anticipate the way he would feel when he saw her again. He'd promised himself that he would stay calm and not lose his temper in spite of the emotions that the picture of her in the newspaper had ignited in him. For a moment, he kept that promise.

She was wearing a loose-fitting dress. The color was the blue of her eyes. He couldn't see the fullness of her body beneath the dress, but he could tell from her face, the pinkening of her cheeks and the sparkling in her eyes that she was carrying a child. For a moment he felt his head swim in joy. Then the anger and the pain returned, and in a voice that was strangely quiet he said, "So the newspaper was right. You're pregnant. Is it mine?"

The words hit her like a fist, taking her breath away. "Of course," she answered in a voice as coolly emotionless as his had been.

He'd known that was the answer and couldn't imagine what had possessed him to ask unless he'd wanted to hurt her. "Are you all right?" That's what he'd wanted to know, but now he realized that it sounded like no more than an apology for what had come before.

"I'm fine," she answered. "The baby's fine."

Nick was torn, with anger and joy so mixed in him that there was no way to get a clear grip on either. First one emotion surfaced in his questions, then another.

"Why the hell didn't you tell me, Ella? I'm the baby's father. Why didn't you tell me?"

"I was going to," she answered quietly. "I tried to reach you yesterday."

"Before that, Ella. Why didn't you tell me before?" He clenched his fists, willing himself to stay calm, not to reach out and shake the truth from her.

"You weren't even in the country, Nick. I couldn't reach you, and then—"

"Stop it, Ella. You could have reached me if you'd wanted to. Gavin could have gotten hold of me. You could have left a message at the State Department. You could have left a message with your service, for God's sake, after I finally got home. Why didn't you?"

Ella had been standing next to the examining table, but her legs were growing weak, and she sank into a chair nearby. Nick remained standing at the door as she explained, "Because I didn't know how you'd react. That is, I was afraid I *did* know."

"How could you know, Ella? I don't even know myself."

Ella smiled tentatively, and Nick saw in her eyes this time not innocence but serenity. He wanted to step across the room and take her in his arms, hold her, kiss her, make her realize that they needed to be together. Once that had solved all their problems; now he knew it wasn't enough. He leaned back against the door-jamb; the distance between them seemed as wide as the Pacific.

"Maybe I didn't know how you'd react," she said, "but I knew what your solution would be."

"Of course you did, Ella. There's only one solution, to take you and the baby back home." He couldn't bite back the words.

Ella looked at him evenly, her face still calm. "This is home for me right now, Nick," she said firmly.

He didn't answer immediately. Just a few days before he'd tried to see more clearly what Ella was all about; he'd promised himself to try to understand her, but it was so damned difficult, because there didn't seem to be any choice here. She was going to have his baby.

"What do you want, Ella?" he asked.

"I want you to stay here for a few days—" Deliberately, she misunderstood his question.

"That's a certainty," he said, looking at her long and hard with his dark, penetrating eyes but not challenging her.

"There's an extra room upstairs," she told him.

Nick didn't blink. "Fine," he said. "I didn't bring any luggage, but I stopped and bought a few things at Paradise Cove before the boat left."

"I'll have someone take them upstairs for you," Ella answered. "After dinner, maybe you'd like to have a tour of the facility."

"I'd like that very much," he answered, remaining as formal as she. It was obvious she wasn't willing to talk now. "Will you have dinner with me down at the beach restaurant?"

Ella shook her head. "I think it would be best to dine here with the staff tonight, Nick."

"Fine." He still hadn't touched her, hadn't even made a move toward her. Something about Ella's demeanor had stopped him. She was different, in charge, confident, and, what's more, he thought, she was happy. That pleased him and at the same time made him jealous. He hadn't been able to make her happy. Work in the clinic had done what he couldn't do.

He paused over that thought and realized there was something much more important. The baby. That glow on her face was there because she was carrying his child. He could tell how much she wanted the child, and he shared her feelings. But they were still going in different directions when it came to the future for them, for *all* of them.

Dinner was pleasant, with the Dunnes putting everyone at ease, telling Nick all about the clinic, voicing their relief that they'd left the fast-lane life of Los Angeles behind for the challenge of Kikao. Their strong feelings on that last subject were shared by Ella. Nick listened quietly, absorbing every word, letting himself open up to what he was hearing. So quickly, Kikao had become Ella's home, just as surely as Fox Haven was his.

They lingered over coffee while the staff cleared away the dishes and Nick complimented everyone on the meal.

"We're getting there," Susan said. "Our cook is marvelous, but when we're ready to have the patients staying at the clinic, she's going to have to go easy on the sauces. Except for the fish, everything we ate tonight was incredibly rich."

"When do you think you'll be set up for long-term care?" Nick asked.

Ella answered that question with enthusiasm. "In less than a month, we hope. You'll find out how far along we are when I take you on the tour."

Nick tried to acquiesce gracefully. The last thing he wanted was a tour, but Ella was determined. This was her turf; she was proud of it, and there was no point in forcing a showdown. At least, he thought philosophically, they'd have a chance to be alone.

From what he'd already seen, Nick expected the clinic to be in good shape, but he was amazed to find that it was much more. Ella led him down the hall past the comfortable waiting room, a small laboratory and X-ray facility and two completely equipped examining rooms. Then they crossed to the other wing, which was still being remodeled.

"We'll have two private rooms and a ward that will accommodate six patients," Ella told him as they stepped around the building materials so he could see the progress being made. Walls had been knocked out to enlarge the rooms that were being completely redesigned, making use of the original woodwork and oak beams.

"It's going to have a lot of charm, isn't it?" Ella asked.

He saw what she meant. "Not like an antiseptic hospital room at all," he agreed. "You've kept the feeling of a villa. It's beautiful, Ella, and you should be very proud of yourself." All at once Nick felt nervous, afraid of her strength and her certainty. He was beginning to wonder if he'd lost her.

Ella didn't notice anything in his look as she talked about the clinic. "Both of the doctors we've hired have training in radiology and pathology, so we'll be able to handle basics. Nothing fancy right away..."

"But so much more than they've ever had," Nick said.

"Yes. For the first time in my life, I've accomplished something on my own, Nick. Not that I didn't have lots of help, beginning with the trustees of Cody's estate all the way through the Dunnes, who are the backbone of the clinic. But it was my idea, and now I can see it all here. It's in the stone and mortar of the building and the flesh and blood of the doctors. It's working."

Nick felt that same fear come over him again. "I've always believed in you," he told her.

"Now I believe in myself. I think I can do anything." There was a long pause as they retraced their steps. "Even rear a baby on my own," she added just as they got back to the main hall.

"No, Ella," he said, stopping short and taking her arm. "This is our baby. Ours. We have to find a way to bring him up together."

228 Stairway to the Moon

"It could be a *her*, Nick," she reminded him, "but you're right. We do have to work something out."

"That's why I'm here, Ella, to put an end to this separation, which is sure as hell none of my doing."

Ella looked at him sharply, and Nick realized his anger, which had been simmering since he'd first seen the newspaper, was on the verge of breaking through. Tiredly, he ran his fingers through his hair. "Sorry, I've got jet lag on top of jet lag. Probably nothing I say will make sense tonight."

"I'm tired, too," Ella agreed almost too quickly. "Let me take you to your room. We'll have tomorrow to talk."

Nick followed her up the stairs, thinking that so far he'd gained nothing, but at least he was with Ella, instead of thousands of miles away.

His room was large and airy and looked out across the hills. Ella had decorated all the bedrooms with furniture made on Kikao, solid and attractive. There was a bright quilt on the four-poster bed. Nick assured Ella that he would be comfortable, and as she left he kissed her lightly on the forehead, taking care not to include his feelings in the gesture.

For a brief moment, Nick thought she moved toward him a little, but he couldn't be sure, and before he could say a word, she'd slipped away.

Ella's hands were shaking as she undressed for bed, and she knew why. Being so close to Nick after aching for him all these weeks had been almost more than she could bear. What made it worse was that Nick had been waiting for her to give in and fall into his arms. Then everything would have been the way it was before. She was sure that's how he perceived their situation, but it was so much more complicated. She was not the woman he'd met on that boat ride to Kikao, and things would never be the same. As she tossed and turned waiting for sleep to come, Ella couldn't imagine that tomorrow would bring a solution.

Nick slept fitfully and awoke at four in the morning, not so much with jet lag as with anxiety. Everything he'd wanted to say to Ella had been lost in the excitement of the clinic. He'd told her he was proud, and he was. He'd told himself that he was trying to understand her, and he was. But damn it, he thought, she was just going to have to face his feelings about their future.

At six o'clock, Nick tapped lightly on her door. Ella was already up and had just stepped from the shower. She answered in her robe, expecting it to be Susan with an emergency downstairs.

"Nick, I—" she said, pulling the robe close around her full body.

"Don't, Ella," he demanded, catching her hand. "Don't be shy with me. Not now when you're carrying our child." His voice had softened, and he stepped into the room, still holding her hand.

Ella didn't move. Her hand was by her side, but he lifted it until both her hand and his rested on her abdomen. "Just let me touch you," he begged. "Let me touch the life we've made together." Nick spread his fingers across her ample stomach and thought he felt a slight fluttering beneath his palm.

"Is he kicking?" he asked, his throat dry, the words barely audible.

She nodded, unable to speak.

"Oh, Ella, Ella," he said. His arms went around her then, gently, almost reverently, and at last he felt her next to him as he'd yearned to feel her for so long. He buried his hands in her hair and found her lips with his.

It was such a complete and loving kiss that it took both of them by surprise. Ending it, they held on to each other, nearly laughing and nearly crying.

"We have to talk, Ella."

"I know," she said. "It's time."

They sat down on her high bed, side by side, leaning back against the pillows. Nick said, "Remember when we were here together and you first saw that pitiful little clinic down by the port?"

"Yes," she said. "That's when my dream began."

He put his arm around her, holding her close. "I told you yesterday that I believed in you all along."

Ella looked up at him.

"Well, I did believe, Ella. I knew you could do anything you put your mind to. I knew you could leave La Casa, but somehow I didn't think you would."

"What about the clinic?" she asked.

"I didn't know you'd get so involved. You've achieved what you set out to do."

"Well, I'm part of the way there."

"Ella, it's all set up, operating smoothly. Now it's time to get on with our lives."

Ella found herself tensing.

"Listen to me, Ella," he said lovingly but firmly. "I loved you from the minute I saw you. I've been patient. Well, maybe not so patient. If I'd known you were here I'd certainly have come sooner."

"I know that. You'd have come with an ultimatum. Marry you. Become the ambassador's wife.
That's why I didn't tell you right away."

"I know now," he said, "and it's time for you to
hear me out. I've wanted you all along, and I've
wanted a child with you. Now I'm damned if I'll give
up without a fight."

"Why do we have to fight?" she asked.

"You mean we don't? You'll marry me and come
home?"

"Nick, I—"

"Answer me, Ella."

She turned in his arms and looked up at him. "I
love you, Nick. I really do, with all my heart."

"Well, then?"

"I'm not sure I can do it your way."

"You don't even know what my way is, Ella. I've
turned down the ambassadorship," he told her.

"But it's what you wanted, what you worked for."

"There's plenty of other work I can do under the
aegis of the State Department, and I didn't want to be
overseas again for years with you having to fit into life
as an ambassador's wife. I knew you wouldn't want
that, either. It would have been too much like your life
with Cody, living in a fishbowl, bending your needs to
mine."

He understood that, Ella thought, her spirits lifting; maybe he would understand the rest. "You turned
it down for me?"

"For *us*, Ella. I want us to come first, more than
ever now that the baby's on the way." He kissed her

gently, luxuriating in the feel of just holding her again. "You agree with that, don't you?"

She kissed him back. "I agree."

"Then let's go home, Ella, back to the States, back to Fox Haven. We can take our time with the next step in our lives, but the baby needs to be—"

"Born at Fox Haven? I'm not sure I agree, Nick. I'm not sure I want to go back to Fox Haven and have our baby there and enroll him in Princeton and—"

"All right," he said almost angrily. "You have the upper hand, Ella. I can't force you, but I will tell you this, I'm not going to walk away. I'll do everything I can to see that you and my baby come back with me. I can take care of you both, Ella. I *want* to take care of you," he said determinedly.

Ella smiled then, a sweet, sad smile of regret. "Oh, Nick, darling Nick, you still don't understand."

Chapter 12

It was possible that she'd explained enough, she thought, and he just couldn't or wouldn't understand. Ella didn't have time to find out the next day, and after that their lives were settled by fate.

"It sounds like they're expecting the storm to develop into a typhoon," Doug was saying as Ella and Nick went down to breakfast.

Susan looked concerned. "We should have taken the warnings more seriously."

"Unfortunately, living in California didn't give us the best training in typhoon preparedness. Now if this were an earthquake..." Doug was trying to make light of their situation, but his gaze was directed outside, where the palm trees were already swaying threateningly.

"So Typhoon Marie is going to be a reality," Nick observed as he and Ella sat down at the table.

"How *do* we prepare for it?" Ella asked, not knowing much more than the Dunnes.

Nick answered that with a question of his own. "Is there a basement in this building?"

"No," Doug told him, "but there's a pantry that was built with a double wall for coolness."

"That should be safe if you have emergency equipment. You'll need to check the generator, round up candles and oil lamps and fill all the available bottles and jars with water. Fortunately, you don't have overnight patients to worry about. What news did you get on the radio?"

"It started as a tropical depression over Fiji," Doug told Nick. "Looked like it might die out in the Pacific. This morning the forecast was changed. It seems to be developing into a full-fledged typhoon. The barometer's falling like crazy."

Nick got up and went to the window. He could see the whitecaps far out in the Pacific. Nearer the shore, they were boiling up into ugly gray waves, and hovering just above them were thick, menacing clouds that hadn't burned away. Nick had experience dealing with natural disasters of every kind. He didn't like the looks of this one, and he knew what he had to do. First, he'd make sure the Dunnes were prepared.

He went back to the table and instructed Doug, "Get all your available help together right away. You have extra lumber, don't you?"

"Plenty of it," Doug responded.

"The windows need to be boarded up. How long did the radio say we have?"

"About four hours unless it changes course," Doug answered as he started out of the room to round up the staff.

"Ella, you and I are leaving," Nick said, putting his hand on her shoulder. "We'll need to make our plans quickly."

"Nick, no," Ella said.

"Ella—"

She started to get up. "If the typhoon does hit, then I'm going to be needed." She turned to Susan. "There are flashlights and hurricane lamps in the storage room. I'll get them and you can search for the candles."

Susan automatically looked to Nick, as if reluctant to accept Ella's help without a word from him.

"I'm taking Ella home," Nick told her firmly. His hand was still on Ella's shoulder, and she hadn't tried to get up again. "The seas are high, but a boat still can get across to the big island. I imagine planes will still be flying, away from the storm at least."

Susan agreed. "They're probably ferrying the guests at Paradise Cove to the closest safe island."

"From the direction it's taking, that'll probably be Hawaii," Nick said, and Susan agreed.

This conversation was held without consulting Ella. She finally interrupted, saying again, "I'm not leaving."

"You aren't a doctor or a nurse, Ella," Nick responded.

"I'm still useful," she argued. "Susan?" She looked up at her friend expectantly.

"You're about the most useful person on the team," Susan answered. "No one can organize or

handle kids as well as you, but this could be very serious, Ella. I understand why Nick wants you to leave.
In fact, as your doctor, I'd recommend it."

"Are you staying?" Ella asked pointedly.

"Yes," Susan answered.

"Well, then, so am I."

Doug had come back into the dining room. "I've
put everyone to work," he said before he noticed the
stillness at the table. "What is it?"

"They want me to leave," Ella answered.

Doug's eyes met his wife's, and he picked up a
message that years of marriage had honed to perfec-
tion. "They're probably right," he said.

"Doug—" Ella began.

Once more, Nick silenced her. "We don't have time
to argue, Ella. Doug and Susan have work to do, and
we need to get out of here." As Nick spoke, Doug and
Susan began their own checklist of duties. There
wasn't time to debate the wisdom of Nick's choice.
The decision had been made for them, and there were
other, more pressing matters to attend to.

"Let me know when you're ready," Doug said as he
and Susan left the room, "and I'll drive you to the
dock."

"No more than fifteen minutes," Nick responded.

He and Ella were alone, with Nick calm, Ella determined. Her face was flushed; her eyes were flashing.

"We're leaving, Ella, and that's final."

"You're being overly cautious, Nick," she argued.
"Doug and Susan are staying."

"Doug and Susan aren't pregnant. This is dangerous for you and the baby."

"I'm sure there are other pregnant women on the island."

"They live here, Ella," he said curtly. "They have no choice." Then Nick calmly took her hand and looked down at her, speaking in a low, controlled voice. "We don't have much time to get out, and I'm not going to take any chances. I've been in hurricanes and typhoons. I know what can happen. It's not a pretty sight, trees uprooted, roofs blown off houses, whole towns leveled."

"I know it can be terrible." She was wavering, but her innate sense of bravery still persisted. "If the typhoon does hit, they'll need all the help they can get on Kikao."

Nick sat down beside her, still holding her hand. "One of the reasons I love you is because of your compassion, Ella. You always think of others, but now I want you to think of yourself and just *one* someone else. Our baby."

Ella felt the tears forming in her eyes.

"It's not fair to risk that innocent life. That's why I have to get you off the island. Come with me now," he pleaded, "while there's still time. We'll fly to safety until it blows over. Please, Ella. I could never forgive myself if anything happened to you." He reached for her, and she clung to him desperately, understanding everything now. He was afraid, not for himself but for her and the baby. She'd never known him to express fear, but she heard it in his voice and felt it in his touch. He was afraid he wouldn't be able to protect her from what might happen.

"I'd do anything to keep you and the baby safe, Ella," he told her. "I'd give my own life gladly, but I don't have that choice. All I can do is take you away."

His arms tightened around her, and she clung to him, feeling the love that flowed between them, warm and powerful. "Tell Doug I'll be ready in ten minutes."

True to her word, Ella had packed a bag and was waiting at the front door of the villa when Doug and Nick brought the jeep around. As they drove through the villages, the islanders were boarding up their huts, preparing for the storm.

"They've been through this before," Nick told her when Ella expressed concern.

"The huts are so rickety," she said. "They'll never withstand typhoon winds."

"If these islands are on the edge of the storm they'll be all right." But Nick, too, was worried; that was apparent in his suggestion to Doug. "When you drive back through, stop and tell them to take shelter in the school and the church. Those buildings are more substantial."

"What about the people up higher, at the village in the hills?" Ella asked.

"There are caves where they can take shelter," Doug assured her, "and we can accommodate many of them in ground-floor rooms at the villa."

Ella still couldn't get over the fact that she was running from the island and going to safety. "I hope they'll leave their huts," she said, knowing the reluctance of a proud people to desert their homes. For many of them, the huts represented their whole world.

"We'll see that they do, Ella," Doug promised.

When they reached the dock, one of the tour boats was preparing to cross to Balboa. "Hurry," the pilot advised when he saw them drive up. "Seas are getting rough. This will be the last trip of the day."

Nick and Ella ran for the boat just as the rains began. With a wave, Doug turned the jeep around and headed back toward the hills.

They were the only two passengers, and as the skies blackened, the pilot began to look doubtful. "Only two of you," he said.

"Don't worry," Nick said. "We'll both pay double fares."

That was enough encouragement. The pilot headed for the engine room, yelling instructions for his mate to cast off. They were on the way.

With his arm around Ella Nick stood by the rail, listening to the boat's motor turning over. There was a frown on his face, which she didn't see as she admitted, "I'm glad we're leaving. For the baby's sake, it was a good idea." She looked up at him. "Thank you, Nick."

"It may be too soon for thanks," he answered.

The engine had turned over again and again, but it hadn't caught. Because the rain was coming down harder, Nick and Ella went inside and sat on a bench in the galley. By now, she'd heard the sound of the faltering engine, too.

"Nick—" she began.

He quieted her with a gesture of his hand. "Wait. It may start up." But he'd hardly finished the sentence when he realized the fallacy in it. Leaving Ella in the galley, he made his way quickly to the engine room.

The mate was already there, and the trouble had been discovered. Ella could hear Nick berating the captain. She knew immediately that they weren't making the crossing in this boat.

"When did you make the trip last?" he asked.

"Two days ago," came the answer.

"You've been sitting here in dock for two days, and you didn't even check the engine?" Nick's voice was raised in anger, but he didn't even wait for a response.

Returning to the galley, he instructed Ella to wait there for him.

"I'm going to find another boat."

"You won't have any luck today," the captain called after Nick.

He was right. After a long trek up and down the dock in the torrential rain, Nick returned to the boat and collapsed on the bench next to Ella.

"I'm sorry," she said.

He looked at her with a frown, and then put his arm around her shoulder. He was wearing a lightweight windbreaker. It was soaked through, and his arm left a damp mark on Ella's jacket. "There's nothing for you to be sorry about," he assured her.

"I should have left when you told me to, and we'd have been here in plenty of time to get another boat."

"Maybe and maybe not," he said without rancor. "It doesn't matter now."

"What'll we do?" Ella asked. For the first time, she was beginning to feel fear.

"Call Doug and get him back down here to pick us up."

Once again, they seemed to be a step too late, a step behind the elements. By the time they got to the only phone on the dock, it was already out. "The rains must have washed down a line," Nick said, taking Ella by the hand. "We'll have to find our own transportation."

Almost an hour passed before Nick located the owner of the seaside restaurant and commandeered his jeep. It was a lost hour, an hour that made all the difference. By the time they began to climb into the hills, the winds hit. The jeep was brought to a standstill. By turning at an angle, Nick was able to get a little farther up the rutted road, which was fast becoming a mud slide. Ella could hear the wind raging. The sound was like a deep muffled cry, and she felt the hairs on the back of her neck standing up straight. She'd never heard a noise like the noise of the wind tearing at the jeep. It filled her with terror.

Nick turned again, maneuvering against the wind as he might have tacked in a boat, using all the skill he possessed. It wasn't enough. At the last turn before reaching the peak of the hill, the wind caught in the top of the jeep, tore at the canvas and ripped it off.

Ella felt the power of the wind that before she'd only heard. It was so sudden and so strong that she thought her head would be ripped from her shoulders. She buried her face against Nick's chest. He put his arm around her and held her for the briefest moment before shouting to her.

As close as they were, in each other's arms, Ella only caught a few of his words. "Hold—fast—look—for—cave."

The wind blew away the rest, but she understood, and as he pushed open the door of the jeep, Ella fell out with him. Holding each other tightly around the waist, they stumbled forward, heads down.

It was as dark as the blackest night, and the rain was coming down in almost solid sheets. It pounded on Ella's back and shoulders and head like huge fists. She felt as if she were fighting against some terrible enemy that was determined to beat her down with its rain and rip her limbs away with its wind.

She couldn't see, she couldn't think, and soon she was numb as they fought together toward whatever destination Nick had in mind. She could only hope that through the deluge he saw some place for them to take shelter. She held on to him and depended on him.

Then a noise different from the roaring wind assaulted her ears. It was the sound of branches being torn off trees and crashing to the ground all around them. Just when Ella was sure they were going to be uprooted themselves and tossed through the air like the palm trees, Nick fell forward and she fell with him into a dark, dry place, a cave in the side of the hill.

They held each other but didn't try to talk, because the wind would only swallow their words, and they didn't have the energy anyway. They could only huddle in the dark and wait for the storm to pass. When at last a calm descended on them, Ella looked out into the still black morning. "Is it over?" she asked.

"No, not yet," he told her. "The eye is passing through, and soon the wind will build up again."

She waited, not afraid now but expectant. She could feel Nick's body against hers, his arms around her, holding her, protecting her. Once, she'd fought that protection; now she was grateful for it. She moved slightly so that she could slip her arms around his neck and hold him close.

"Are you all right?" he asked over the wind that had picked up again in intensity.

"I'm more than all right. I'm with you."

"I swear I won't let anything happen to you," he told her.

"I'm not afraid," Ella said softly, so softly that he almost didn't hear her over the whine of the wind. "How can I be afraid when I'm with the man I love?"

Then the earth seemed to shake with the storm's passion, and they held on to each other, not in desperation but in trust and love.

The wind was stronger now than it had been before, so fierce that even in the protection of the cave, they had to cover their eyes to avoid being blinded by flying debris. Just when Ella thought the roar could get no louder, something stirred above them, and a large tree was uprooted and thrown against the opening of the cave, closing them in with a mound of dirt and roots.

"Will we be able to get out?" Ella screamed to him.

He didn't answer for what seemed like an eternity, and then he asked her, "Can you feel the wind coming through?"

"Yes, yes!" she answered.

"We're not blocked completely; I'll get you out," he promised, and she knew he would.

What seemed like days later but was in reality no more than a few hours, Ella awoke in her own bed. The room was bright. She got up and went to the window. What she saw brought tears to her eyes. It looked like a war zone, flattened not by man's bombs but by nature's winds. Trees were torn from the ground, sheds and outbuildings overturned, some blown yards away from where they'd originally stood, others demolished. A large section of roof had been blown off the villa and the construction ripped away. On the second floor only the wing with their bedrooms was intact, but the ground floor had withstood the typhoon with minor damage, although an outside wall had collapsed, injuring several people.

The villagers' homes were another matter. She imagined that those in the direct line of the gale and not built of concrete had been destroyed. Ella knew there was work to be done. She pulled on her clothes and hurried downstairs.

The waiting room was filled, and Susan was standing in the middle of a crowd, trying to determine which of the injured to treat next. She grabbed a small child who appeared to have a broken leg and lifted him up while the others clutched at her.

"Ella," she said, "thank God you're up." Susan gave her a big hug.

"I didn't want to lie down at all, but Nick insisted, and I fell asleep."

"You needed the rest," Susan said, "but now we need your help."

Ella assessed the situation quickly. "I'll take care of the minor injuries in here and try to get everyone calmed down."

"Great," Susan said as she headed down the hall. "Doug's almost ready for the next patient. Send in the most seriously hurt first."

"I will," she answered, and then called after Susan. "Do you know where Nick is?"

"He drove out in the jeep to bring back those who can't get here on their own," Susan answered as she disappeared into an examining room.

Ella was bandaging a little girl's leg in the waiting room when Nick returned. He stood for a moment in the doorway and watched. The room was quiet. She'd calmed the children, reassured the adults and made a big pot of coffee with the fresh water they'd stored. It was well after dark, and she'd lit the room with stubs of candles that gave an almost festive aura to the occasion. Two of the smallest children were singing a song Ella had taught them as she worked. It was a peaceful scene in which Ella Butler was the center. Her serenity was felt everywhere.

"I love you," he said softly.

Ella looked up with a smile. "It's mutual," she whispered over the dark head of the girl in her lap. She'd cleaned the cut, the bandage was in place and the child had fallen asleep. Ella put the little girl in her mother's arms and walked over to Nick.

"If you can spare a moment, I'd like to see you alone," he said.

She nodded and took his hand. "There's no one in the kitchen right now."

The room was dark. The one candle that had been burning there had been requisitioned by the doctors, but Nick could see her vaguely in the moonlight that streamed through the window. She was more beautiful now than ever before. He thought about the way they'd huddled together in that cave until the typhoon passed and then driven in the mud-soaked jeep back to the villa, where he'd put her to bed. He wasn't surprised that she'd slept only a couple of hours. Ella's commitment to the island and its people was total. His only job was to keep her from getting overtired, and he was determined to watch after her, since she wouldn't think of herself.

"How was it out there?" she asked.

"Bad," he answered honestly. "A lot of devastation."

"Some were killed?"

"I'm afraid so, Ella."

She shook away her despair. "The real work is just beginning for us," she said, "to take care of the survivors."

"Yes, I know." He brushed the hair back from her forehead and stole a moment to kiss her softly on each eyelid. "I brought five more people back in the jeep. Will you help me get them into the waiting room?"

"Let's go," Ella answered, kissing him quickly on the lips.

That was their last touch for many hours, but not their last contact, for they worked side by side with Susan, Doug and the two doctors as well as other staff people who hadn't been hurt in the typhoon. It was dawn of the next day before Nick finally got Ella back to bed again. This time he lay down beside her, and in a few moments they were both asleep.

When she woke up he was standing at the foot of her bed. "I've brought you hot tea and toast," he said. "It's all I could scrounge up in the kitchen."

"It looks wonderful." She took the tray from him and as he watched, amused, hungrily devoured every crumb and drank the tea while it was still piping hot.

"I'll get some more," he said.

"No." She stopped him. "Later. I was famished, but I'm all right now. Stay here and talk to me for a few minutes."

"Gladly." He sat down beside her on the bed. "You look ravishing. A little grimy but nevertheless..."

Ella laughed. "I'd hate to see myself in the mirror. A mixture of dust, dirt, mud and blood, I suspect."

"That's about right," Nick said, laughing. "But we have enough water for you to wash up."

"Wonderful," Ella said. She was beginning to feel the energy flow back into her veins. They'd survived the worst. Although months of rebuilding lay ahead, the immediate problems were over. "We did it," she said.

"Yes, we did, and I don't think it would have been possible without you, Ella. I guess fate was on the side of the islanders when that damned skipper couldn't get his motor started."

Ella laughed. "I'm so glad we didn't get out. Now I feel more a part of the island than ever."

Nick looked at her thoughtfully. He'd made a decision of his own during the night, one that would have amazed him only a few days before.

Ella had seen the look in his eyes but hadn't interpreted it. She went on. "I came here to prove something, Nick. At first to myself and then to you." She smiled the old impish smile he loved so much. "Then I stayed on because Kikao began to mean something very important to me."

"I realize that, Ella."

"It wasn't just the challenge of proving myself anymore. It was an attachment that I never thought I'd find. A place to belong."

He touched her face gently. "I guess I didn't realize what it was like for you not to have a home. Seeing you here has made me understand a little better. But I must say, it's also scared the hell out of me. I was afraid something would happen to you and my son." He leaned his head thankfully against her stomach, and Ella ran her hands through his thick dark hair.

"It could be a girl, Nick," she reminded him.

"Son or daughter, either is too precious to lose."

"I knew you'd take care of us. I was never afraid; panicked maybe, when it looked like we wouldn't find a place out of the wind, but not afraid." She continued to stroke his hair, feeling a surge not just of thankfulness but of love so complete she couldn't find a way to express it.

Nick answered thoughtfully, "What really scared me from the first moment I arrived is that you might not need me, that I might not be able to take care of you the way I wanted to."

"I did need you, Nick, and I do need you, but I hope you can understand that I need to have my own place in the world, my own niche here at the clinic. I can't walk away from it, Nick, not now."

Ella paused, waiting anxiously for his reaction, and then he told her what he'd decided only hours before.

Epilogue

Grace Nicole Manning kicked happily in her crib and reached for the colorful mobile above her head. Ella looked up from the letter she was writing and smiled as Nick came up the steps of the porch to the villa. He dropped a kiss on her forehead before going over to pick up his daughter.

When he tossed her high into the air, the baby squealed with delight. "I can't believe I ever wanted a son," Nick said. "Nikki just may be the most beautiful child I've ever seen." He gave his daughter a big kiss, and once more she laughed, to her father's obvious joy.

"I'm sending more pictures in this letter to your parents," Ella told him.

"That should satisfy them at least until their visit."

"Do you think the research center will be finished by then?" Ella asked. In the distance she could hear the constant roar of the bulldozers.

"I hope so. We're making great progress in spite of the time and money that goes into meeting the typhoon standards. But at least we'll be able to guarantee the safety of every patient."

Ella leaned back in her chair and looked out across the hills of Kikao. The scene had never failed to lift her spirits, from the first time she and Nick had come to the island. They'd been strangers then. Now they were a part of it all, the people, the land and, most important, the clinic, which was turning into a top medical center.

The research center for tropical diseases was under construction, to be headed by a Nobel prize-winning doctor from New Zealand. The little island of Kikao was on the map, and Ella Manning gloried in the publicity they were receiving. The Ella Butler days were over; now the journalists treated her with respect, paid attention not to how she looked but to what she had to say.

Nick put the baby back in her crib and joined his wife. "I have a meeting in Balboa next week with the rest of the committee. We should get final approval then," he told her.

Ella poured two glasses of iced tea and handed one to Nick. "Do you ever regret it?"

He raised a dark eyebrow and looked at her, a little surprised. "Regret what, marrying you? Having the most beautiful daughter in the world? Living in paradise?"

Ella laughed. "No, staying here on Kikao and heading up the international agency that's building our center."

"It's probably the most exciting job I've ever had," he answered.

"It's not Athens or Rome," she reminded him.

"No, it's not," he admitted.

"It's not an ambassadorship."

"Right again," he agreed, "but I've lived in Athens and in Rome. I lived there alone, Ella. Anywhere I live with you and Nikki is paradise to me. I'm just doubly blessed that the real paradise happens to be located here on Kikao."

"What about the ambassadorship?" she asked again. Ella often worried that Nick hadn't fulfilled what both he and his family believed to be his potential, but she'd never broached the subject before, because she'd been a little afraid of the answer. Now, after sharing his life as Mrs. Nicholas Manning, she was more confident.

Nick put down his glass and reached for Ella, lifting her onto his lap. "An ambassadorship may still be possible someday if the whole team is for it, you and me and Nikki. Right now nothing could be as exciting as what we have here, what we've built together."

"We're a good team, aren't we?"

He kissed her thoroughly and slowly. "We always were."

Ella snuggled her head against his neck, her hand caressing the edge of his hairline. "Listen," she whispered. "I have an idea."

"This could be trouble," he teased her.

"There's a group of huts down near the dock, at the water's edge..."

"Where the moon's reflection creates a stairway," he added.

"Yes," she said, sighing in his arms. "A stairway to the moon."

"I'm told the huts were all rebuilt after the typhoon," he said.

"With every modern convenience but without losing the romantic feeling they had for one couple eons ago."

"You mean that spring night?" he asked, nibbling at her ear.

Ella nodded. "The night when..."

Nick grinned as he looked over at the baby playing in her crib. "Yes," he said. "I think that was Nikki's beginning."

"She'll be a year old soon," Ella said. "She's probably already thinking about a little brother..."

"I've been thinking about that, too," Nick said, "but don't forget what you used to tell me, Ella. It could be a girl."

*   *   *   *   *

Silhouette Special Edition

THE O'HURLEYS! CHANTEL'S STORY

from
Nora Roberts

Skin Deep
Available September 1988

The third in an exciting new series about the lives and
loves of triplet sisters—

In May's *The Last Honest Woman* (SE #451), Abby
finally met a man she could trust...then tried to
deceive him to protect her sons.

In July's *Dance to the Piper* (SE #463), it took some
very fancy footwork to get reserved recording mogul
Reed Valentine dancing to effervescent Maddy's
tune....

In *Skin Deep* (SE #475), find out what kind of heat it
takes to melt the glamorous Chantel's icy heart.
Available in September.

Silhouette Intimate Moments

COMING
NEXT MONTH

#257 BUT THAT WAS YESTERDAY—Kathleen Eagle

Sage Parker had a busy life on the reservation, rebuilding his ranch and struggling to teach his people the value of the old tribal ways. Then Megan McBride became his boss and turned his familiar world upside down. She was everything a woman could be, and before Sage could back away, he realized she was also the only thing he needed.

#258 CODY DANIELS' RETURN—Marilyn Pappano

Border Patrol agent Cody Daniels had never wanted to see Mariah Butler again, but when she became a suspect in his latest investigation, all his old feelings for her resurfaced. His sense of duty wouldn't let him clear her without question, but his heart wouldn't let him betray the woman he was beginning to love all over again.

#259 DANGEROUS CHOICES—Jeanne Stephens

Abby Hogan had believed for years that Jason Cutter was a cold, uncaring man—until her job as an insurance investigator brought them together again. Abby soon discovered that she was interested in Jason, but old habits die hard, and only a dangerous confrontation with some real villains made her realize that what she felt was love.

#260 THIS ROUGH MAGIC—Heather Graham Pozzessere

Wolves were howling and the Halloween moon was full when Carly Kiernan came to the castle and met the count, a fascinating man who dressed in black and disappeared at will. Carly knew that everything would seem different in the light of day, but the morning only brought another question: why was she falling in love with a man whose very name was a mystery?

AVAILABLE THIS MONTH:

ATTRACTIVE, SPACE SAVING BOOK RACK

Display your most prized novels on this handsome and sturdy book rack. The hand-rubbed walnut finish will blend into your library decor with quiet elegance, providing a practical organizer for your favorite hard-or soft-covered books.

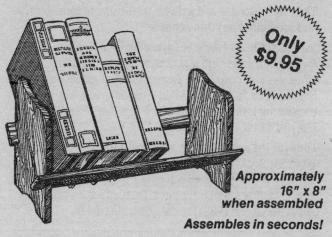

Only $9.95

Approximately 16" x 8" when assembled

Assembles in seconds!

To order, rush your name, address and zip code, along with a check or money order for $10.70* ($9.95 plus 75¢ postage and handling) payable to *Silhouette Books*.

Silhouette Books
Book Rack Offer
901 Fuhrmann Blvd.
P.O. Box 1396
Buffalo, NY 14269-1396

Offer not available in Canada.

BKR-2A

*New York and Iowa residents add appropriate sales tax.

Silhouette Intimate Moments

WHEN OPPOSITES ATTRACT

Roberta Malcolm had spent her life on the Mescalero ranch. Then Hollywood—and Jed Pulaski—came to Mescalero, and suddenly everything changed.

Jed Pulaski had never met anyone like Rob Malcolm. Her forthright manner hid a woman who was beautiful, vibrant—and completely fascinating. But Jed knew their lives were as far apart as night from day, and only an all-consuming love could bring them together, forever, in the glory of dawn.

Look for Jed and Roberta's story in *That Malcolm Girl*, IM #253, Book Two of Parris Afton Bonds's Mescalero Trilogy, available this month only from Silhouette Intimate Moments. Then watch for Book Three, *That Mescalero Man* (December 1988), to complete the trilogy.
